# Testimonies of The Trap

A NOVEL BY Myriah

# Acknowledgements

Maybe you've heard of me or read my work. Maybe you haven't. Either way, I want to acknowledge YOU for taking a chance on little ol' me. I can only pray that Jeryn's story speaks to your heart. Ultimately, the readers are the reason that I do what I do. Your reviews, your constructive criticism, all of it I take in, in hopes of bettering myself and my craft. I hope that you can see the development in every single one of my books.

To my mommy, life is hard without you here. Every moment of every day I miss you and I can only pray that the day we see eachother again will come quickly. I love you, woman.

To the newest angel and the name inspiration for my main character, my father, Jaron J. Westbrooks. I hope that you get the peace there that you couldn't get here. I love you forever and forever daddy. I can only hope I'm making you proud.

*"You know you're in love when you can't fall asleep because reality is finally better than your dreams."* –Dr. Seuss

# *Chapter One:*

*"Baby, it's only been one night. Feel like it's been a week."*
*–Daya*

My feet froze as I stared down the aisle at the gruesome sight before me. I was unable to move. It felt like all of the oxygen had been sucked out of my body. This man's engagement ring was hung around my neck as a public display of his love and affection towards me, yet I wasn't the woman standing in front of him, taking his name. My eyes stung with hatred as I realized Jalen had been playing me this entire time. Three years, three months, six days and eleven hours. All of it had been a lie. If he thought that I was just going to let him get away with this, he must have clearly forgotten who I was.

"Forreal, Jalen?" I yelled, storming down to where the happy couple was standing. Everyone was staring at me, but I didn't give one single fuck. "I thought you loved me, Jalen?" I shouted. The bride stepped towards me with tears in her eyes, probably trying to shut me up, but I shot her a look that warned her not to come any closer to me. Her best bet was to stay as far away from me as she could get. I could tell she was straight from the suburbs, but I was a real hood bitch, not one of these stuck up hoes that were sitting in this church. She had no chance against me. Jalen was clearly surprised to see me standing there and stepped forward to restrain me, but I wasn't about to let him touch me. Landing a quick but painful punch to his lip, I enjoyed watching blood pour out of his mouth and onto his white tax. *He wouldn't be getting that stain out anytime soon.* "You will regret this. I promise you." I warned him, quietly enough so that only the two of us could hear and Jalen's eyes nearly bulged out of his head. He knew exactly what I was talking about. I am Jeryn Alexah January, the daughter of Jerry Armani January, Jr. Yes, *that* Jerry. My father had most of the Keys on lock. It didn't matter if it was hoes, drugs, or guns. Anything you needed, he had it. My dad was no longer amongst the living, but that didn't change a fuck thing for us. A problem with me meant a problem with my empire and nobody survived that. All I had to do was put a price on his head and one of my shooters would definitely handle it.

Walking out of the church, I kept my head held high even though my feelings were beyond hurt. I could tell that people were still watching me, trying to figure out what I was going to do next. Everyone had warned me about messing with Jalen. They told me about the problems that he would cause for me. They said he was messy and not shit. But I didn't listen. I broke the vows I had made to my husband, fell in love with Jalen, and all the while was losing myself in the process. Though loving Jalen had given me our beautiful daughter, Jeidyn, that I wouldn't have otherwise, times with him were some of the most turbulent times of my life. Between him and his hoes' drama nonstop, to constantly borrowing money to flip and never paying up, it seemed like the last year with Jalen had been nothing but arguments. Now, he was another bitch's headache and I was okay with that. Or at least I would learn to be one day. But what I wasn't okay with was him and his new hoe driving around in the car that I bought him as a Father's Day present from me and Jeidyn. So I broke it. The windows, the tires, the rims, I broke it all. Even the license plate belonged to me so I broke that bitch too. Then I got in my car and took off with nowhere in mind.

That night, I drove until I couldn't drive any more. I drove like I didn't have two young daughters waiting for me at home to read them a bedtime story and tuck them in for the night. It must have been a sign because I managed to stop driving right in front of one of Jalen and I's properties. I was still furious. Everything that we bought, I wanted it gone and out of my sight. I wanted our investments dissolved. As far as I was concerned, Jalen Louis Hicks no longer existed to me or my daughter. Jalen could have cared less about my feelings or our daughter clearly, so all of the money moves that I put him on were over. Just like my father taught me, it was never good like that to give away free game. Especially to a fuck nigga like Jalen. I couldn't believe how all of this shit played out but after all the trapping I put him on and all the fronts I had given him, it was about time for him to pay up. I could only hope, for his sake, that he had my money. I wanted to walk into the house and destroy everything that reminded me of that punk, but I knew it wouldn't make me feel any better. If anything, wasting my own money would for sure put me in a bad mood. I just wanted to hold Jersei and Jeidyn in my arms while we slept so I turned my car around and started to drive back to my house. At the stoplight, my hand went to my stomach instantly once I felt a flutter. Nobody knew anything because I hadn't announced it publicly yet, but I was seventeen weeks pregnant with Jalen's child. The doctor wasn't for sure yet, but she believed I was having another little girl. Once I pulled up into my driveway, I rushed into the house, kicked off my shoes and smiled. If Jalen thought he was the only one capable of playing these games, he had another thing coming. I was about to turn his world upside down. I had a bad habit of stripping out of my clothes in my home so by the time I made it to my bathroom, I was already clad in my bra and panties. It was my house so I could walk around naked if I wanted to. When I shut the door behind me, I took those off too so that I could bathe in peace. I'd arrived home a little later than I planned so my five-year old daughter, Jersei and my almost two-year old daughter, Jeidyn were already in the bed, fast asleep.

"How are you, baby? How was your meeting?" My husband, Axl, asked as he came into the bathroom. Stripping out of his clothes, he joined me in the tub as we kissed. His eyes were closed, so he couldn't even see me rolling mine. I wasn't even in the mood for whatever games he was about to play with me and nearly threw up when he stuck his tongue in my mouth. He moaned as if my lips tasted good to him, but I wondered how he would feel knowing the reason my lips tasted salty was because I had just spent the last four and a half hours crying over another man. When he tried to kiss on my neck, letting me know what this would lead to, I turned my body away from him. I just didn't feel right making love to him. I felt useless and dirty. I felt like Jalen had just gotten the one thing he wanted from me, but I knew in my heart that he'd gotten a lot more than that. Yes, I had another man's last name, but Jalen Hicks was holding my heart for ransom and now I'd have to watch his blood spill to get it back. Sitting up, Axl sat up too. He could probably sense that something was wrong with me, though I didn't know how. He couldn't tell any other time.

"I need to tell you something, Axl." Taking a deep breath, I shut my eyes and just said what I had to say. "I'm pregnant." Watching his face light up, I knew that had him exactly where I wanted him. After I delivered our stillborn daughter a year after Jersei was born, Axl had stayed trying to get me pregnant. He was ecstatic now and had no idea that the child I was carrying, wasn't even his. Even though I felt slightly guilty, this was nothing compared to what Axl had put me through in the six years that we'd been married. A year into our marriage, right when I found out I was pregnant with my oldest daughter Jersei, some chick came to my house with a baby that looked just like Axl. It turns out that around the time we got married, they had messed around. My daughter had a sister that was only six months older than her.

Pulling up my shirt, he laid his head on my tummy and looked up in surprise when he felt how hard my stomach was. "I'll be twenty weeks on Monday." I answered his question without him ever opening his mouth. I had actually just lied to him, because if I told him the truth, he would know something was up. I had just turned seventeen weeks, but seventeen weeks ago, Axl was away in Rio de Janeiro. He said he was out on business, but I knew he was with that bitch. That was the last time that Jalen and I had been together. Axl's jaw dropped, probably because I had kept my secret for so long, but he continued to kiss all over my stomach. I smiled on the outside, but on the inside, I was irritated and ready for him to get off me. The affection my husband was showing me was too little too late. Maybe I was wrong for doing what I did with Jalen, but so was Axl. My husband's infidelities were no secret to me or anyone around me. Word around the street was that he had been hanging around with some girl named Money and a couple of my friends had even seen them out. At least I wasn't just throwing all of my shit in his face.

# Chapter Two:



Walking up the stairs after a long sleepless night of trying to get Axl off of me, I scowled at the panties thrown carelessly all over the floor and steps. There were dirty dishes in random places and my already weak stomach was turning as I smelled old menstrual pads. If my father were alive, none of these bitches would be trying this. Since it was me, they felt different. That was okay though, because every time they underestimated me, I showed them why they shouldn't. Now, I was about to show them for good and eliminate all confusion, since they'd clearly lost their minds while I took a little break. But I knew my father was looking down on me so I was determined to make him proud. I was the head bitch in charge and it was about time I showed them the power that I held.

"Aye, get the fuck up!" I barked, putting as much bass in my voice as I could muster up. Pounding on the walls, I waited until the girls starting to wake up and then I heard a collection of footsteps before they all fell in line. I guess I had done something right, because they all knew their place.

All six of them, varying in skin color, backgrounds, and attitudes stood in front of me and they already knew what was up. "Who the fuck decided to just lay around this bitch and let it get nasty like this?" I snarled, picking up a pair of discarded panties just to prove my point. They all remained silent but I watched them glance at eachother nervously. "So nobody is going to speak up? You can't hear me or something?" I yelled, now looking at Anastasia. My little Russian bitch. She was down for whatever and that's what I liked about her. With fire red hair and long black acrylics that had clearly grown out, I frowned when I saw how raggedy all of them looked. My father had always prided himself on his girls being "top notch". The best of the best. The finest clothes, they had them. The fanciest cars, my girls drove them. Most importantly, whenever the girls went out, they looked like bags of money. I hadn't been around for a couple of weeks since I was dealing with the whole Jalen situation, and as the glue who kept this whole fucking picture together and the pimp who kept this ship afloat, I knew that was just unacceptable. If my dad were alive, he'd have my head for that. It made me feel bad, but that didn't mean I would let up. I couldn't show them that I sympathized with them, otherwise they would just take advantage of me. My face remained hard and unfazed. Kisa, my youngest but my hardest worker, stepped forward first. Instead of saying anything, she just reached out her hand and deposited cash into my hands. Following her lead, the rest of them did the same and I couldn't get rid of the smile on my face. I counted up every bill and realized that I had over twenty racks in my hands, just from the two weeks that I had been gone.

"We haven't been lazy or slacking, Jeryn. We just been working like we knew you'd want us to. We didn't know what you were doing, so we had to make sure we went out and got it for ourselves." Kisa spoke up bravely. Nodding my head, I took the money in the back to put it in the safe, but I purposely kept some aside. I wasn't like the other "pimps" roaming around in the Key West. I didn't really even consider myself a pimp. I was a boss ass bitch, helping young women come up, just by using what they had between their legs. I watched my girls intently while I trained them and you could see their confidence rising with every trick that they got. I was proud. It was like watching a child grow up and then seeing them go on their own path. But like a strict, overbearing parent, my girls knew not to cross me. It wasn't just that they were scared of me. I made sure they were well taken care of. Everything from their children's daycare, to rent and when their refrigerator was running low, I made sure that it was handled. That's why they were so loyal to me. Not to mention, I only liked dick so they never had to worry about being manhandled like the other pimps in this area. They knew my motive wasn't sexual. I really was just trying to put us all in a position where we could win.

Grabbing the money that I had put aside, I went back into the room where all the girls were waiting patiently. Like I did for them every month, I went down the line and deposited four thousand dollars in each girl's hand. That was enough to pay the rent, gas for their car, their hair, nails, their kids and anything else they needed to handle. If any of the girls needed more, they knew all they had to do was ask for it. After they'd all taken their money and went to handle their business, I noticed Kisa standing around nervously like she had something important to say to me. It wasn't until she noticed everyone else was gone and that's when she walked up to me. I could tell that she was nervous by the way that she fidgeted with her fingers nonstop. Though I had inherited five of the girls from my dad, I operated my business a lot different than him, or anyone else I knew. I didn't have to beat any of my girls down or try to control them with sex. They were loyal to me because at the end of the day, they knew that I would take care of them. Anything that they wanted or needed was theirs. All they had to do was ask and I made it happen. I didn't like to treat my girls different, but Kisa was definitely different than most of them and that's why I didn't relax until I got her on my team. I could tell that something was wrong with her but before she could spit it out, my phone began ringing. I ignored it once but then it began ringing off the hook. I knew it could only be one person, because only one person blew my phone up like that. When I glanced at the screen and saw my sister's name flashing across the screen, I frowned. Part of me wanted to believe Eryanna was just being annoying because she was Eryanna, but the hustler in me knew she wouldn't have called me so many times if it wasn't important.

"What is it, Ery?" I asked, assuming the worst when I could hear her sniffling. I hadn't heard her cry since our dad died. That told me something was seriously wrong. She didn't say anything and she was sniffling so hard, I wasn't sure that she heard me so I repeated myself. "Hello, Eryanna! What is it?" I practically yelled.

"I- I found out who killed dad." She confessed and instead of lightening her load, it only seemed to make her cry harder. I waited for her to speak up but it didn't seem like she was going to say anything. She was just going to make me wonder as if I hadn't done that for the past seven years since our dad was taken from us. I vowed when I found the person who ended my father's life, I would return the favor. It was a hard hit to my family when my dad died, and I'm not just talking about for me and my brother and sister. Aunts, uncles and cousins all felt the same pain we did. But most of all, the January cartel took a major hit with the tragic death of our leader. Money really started slowing down, but with the help of my brother and sister, we got funds coming back in and fast. We weren't my dad, but we did one hell of a job. He would've been proud.

"Are you going to speak up or you gonna make me guess?" I asked after a few moments of silence. Eryanna calmed down enough for me to get an answer, but I wasn't expecting her reply to have my knees buckling under me.

"J… Axl ordered the hit on our dad."

# Chapter Three:



With tears in my eyes, I sat in the driver's seat of my car with the glock in my lap. My finger was steady on the trigger and my heart sped up when I noticed Axl's car was parked on the side. That meant that he was home, so I knew a showdown was coming. Yet, when I walked into the five-bedroom, four bathroom home that my husband and I had built from the ground up, it was silent. Usually, Axl was on the phone talking 'business' to this person or that person. I heard nothing but my footsteps gliding against our marble floors. In my head, all I could hear was my baby sister telling me that Axl, the man I'd been married to and had a daughter with, was the person behind my father's death. Our marriage was supposed to be the truce between the two cartels. Axl went against that, and meant that he had to pay the ultimate price.

It wasn't until I got to the door that led to the basement that I heard voices and some sort of activity. My fingers were just waiting to pull the trigger so I didn't hesitate to march my way down there. Axl just happened to be in a meeting with five other men, two of them were his brothers. They all stopped talking mid-sentence when they heard me come down the steps. I wanted to shoot Axl from where I was standing, but I had to get a better angle so there was no other option but to descend all the way down the stairs. When I did that, I realized I wasn't just in a room of six men. There was a whole room full of soldiers and all of their guns were trained on me. Basically, I'd walked right into a trap and didn't even know it.

Axl knew me so I could tell that he was enjoying watching me figure out what my next move was. But I kept a straight face. There was no way I could give him the satisfaction of seeing me break. All I could do was silently curse myself for not telling anyone where I was so that I could have backup.

"Thanks for joining us, Jeryn. We were just talking about you," Axl taunted me, pausing when the whole room exploded with laughter. For some reason, my flight or fight mode turned off and my brain froze. My whole body froze. I was so mad that tears welled up in my eyes but I forced them to go away. He trailed his finger down my chin but I turned my head in disgust and pushed him off of me. With one snap of his fingers, a couple of men rushed me. They took my gun and held me by the arms. I just knew I was about to die and Axl confirmed that when he pulled out his gun. First, he put the gun to my forehead and I barely blinked an eye. He would have to do better than that. Then he teased me by outlining my face with the butt of his gun, just watching and waiting for me to react. But I knew Axl, probably a lot better than he knew me. Hell, I knew him better than he knew himself. Axl and I had been friends long before we were ever married and before a truce between our families even existed. I guess that's why everyone, including me, assumed it would work. But yet, here we were and my "husband" had a gun to my head. On my way over here, Eryanna had sent me the proof. Screenshots, texts, and pictures detailed the way that Axl had planned this out. There was no doubt in my mind that the man I was married to, murdered my father in cold blood.

I was emotionless until Axl trailed the gun down to my stomach. "You know, Jeryn… I could end this whole problem for us right now…" He snickered, circling his gun around my naval. My eyes started to burn, begging for permission to blink but I fought it. I knew that if I did, the tears would follow soon after. I had no choice but to give in and just as I suspected, I was soon crying like a baby. I had no problem going if it was my time, but I refused to believe that I would be the reason my baby wouldn't get a chance to live. Axl, being the sick bastard he was, started to laugh when he saw how panicked I'd become. "Is it my baby?" he said, quietly enough for the both of us to hear. Unfortunately, the room was dead quiet so everyone heard him. I knew what Axl was capable of if I embarrassed him in a room full of his boys, so I nodded. Tears streamed down my face and I looked in Axl's eyes and told him a bold-faced lie.

"This baby is yours, Axl. I swear to you." I managed to choke out. He seemed satisfied at first, but then that look turned into pity. The last thing I wanted him to do was feel sorry for me, because the first chance that I got, I was going to take him and his whole crew out. However, if pity saved my unborn child's life, I would accept it for now. He seemed to accept my answer. Either that or he really enjoyed seeing me beg. He signaled to his soldiers to let me go. They flung me so far that I lost my footing and tripped.

"Get the fuck out of here Jeryn and I swear to you, you better not be a problem for me. I'm serious. You don't want no smoke with us. You see all these niggas around me? There's a lot more than this." Here's the thing. I knew I was outnumbered already so there was no way that I was going to do something that would get me killed, but I knew Axl's game. He would have me turn around to walk away, just to shoot me in the back. He was a pussy ass nigga, and I could vouch for that. I'd seen it with my own eyes. That wasn't going to happen with me. He would have to work harder than that to take me away from my kids. I eyed the gun that laid on the ground not far from me, but Axl seemed to read my mind. "I'm trying to be nice here. Don't do something stupid." He warned me. For the first time in my life, I heeded a warning and decided to count my losses. For now. But as I fled from the home my husband and I once shared, steadily looking over my shoulder, I forced myself not to think about everything that I was losing and everything that I had to leave behind. In my head though, I knew that this wasn't a loss I was willing to take, but to get what rightfully belonged to me, I would need backup. My first stop was Jalen.

Though Jalen was a fucking liar and a flake when it came to paying me my money back, I would give him credit for one thing. He knew how to flip a dollar into a rack quick, and he was an excellent father to Jeidyn, and even to Jersei. Unlike Axl, he never treated them differently. He had three other children aside from my daughter and he treated all of the girls the same. That's how I knew I could count on Jalen when it came to protecting Jeidyn and our unborn. Despite everything that we had been through, the moment that he saw me and how distraught I was, Jalen dropped everything he was doing to lead me into his office. I was still shaken up about how it had all gone down at the house so when Jalen saw my hands shaking, he gripped me by the wrists to help me sit down.

"Is it, Jeidyn? What's wrong?" he asked frantically. I shook my head, struggling to find the words. I had to be careful how I approached the situation. If I said the wrong thing, Jalen would turn this whole city into a warzone. His dislike for Axl outweighed everything else and sometimes, I was afraid it would get us killed. I still wasn't saying anything and though I wanted to, I enjoyed that my silence was starting to drive him crazy. "Okay? So is it the baby?" I shook my head again and Jalen totally freaked out. "What are you? A fucking mute? Is this some kind of game? I don't have the time to play with you. You come into my wedding starting shit and now you can't talk? You lost your voice from all that screaming?" he snapped loudly, catching me completely off guard. Jalen had never even raised his voice at me. I wasn't scared of him but when he backed me up into a corner, scary thoughts traveled through my mind. Only for a moment though. Then Jalen's aggressive tone caused me to get weak in the knees. Before I knew it, his back was up against the wall while I kissed my way down his body. Pausing at his belt, it only took me seconds before I was flinging it across the room. I needed Jalen like the air flowing through my lungs. I craved his body like I craved warm olives at three o'clock in the morning when nothing was open but legs. At first, Jalen seemed to enjoy it but then he pushed me off of him right when I was about to put him in my mouth. "Nah, nah. Nah. We can't do this. Not 'til you tell me what's going on." Jalen argued as I stared at him in disbelief.

"This is because of her, huh?" I growled, even just the thought of Harmony putting a bad taste in my mouth. Jalen took one look at the look on my face and started to laugh. That only made me madder.

"Yo, you're serious right now?" Jalen chuckled and I could sense that he had so much more to say. I didn't have to wait long. "Yo, on the real baby momma… You know I don't like big words and shit. That's not really my thing… but you realize you sound fucking outrageous right? This is that bullshit y'all bitches be whining about. You don't want me but you don't want nobody else to have me either. That's some sick shit-," Jalen started to go hard on me and I attempted to pause him, but he shut me down. "Nah, Jeryn. No more. I gave you a chance to talk and you didn't say shit. Now it's my turn," he scolded me, shutting me up instantly. "I wanted to give you the world. You and Jeidyn. Even knowing you were married, I stuck around because I was in love with yo' ass. I thought you would eventually see that I was the nigga you needed in your life, the nigga that would change your life. Now you come crying to me, because what?

I was supposed to wait around for you to figure it out? Jeryn, you gave my daughter that fuck nigga's last name knowing she was mine. I can't even claim Jeidyn in public because you lied about who her dad was. Not me." He confronted me. When Jalen told me exactly how he felt, I felt shitty as hell but I knew I deserved it. I had lead Jalen on, knowing I never had any intentions of leaving Axl until I caught feelings. Honestly, if Jeidyn had never been produced, I wasn't sure that Jalen and I would still be together. Ironically, being pregnant with Jeidyn also saved my marriage to Axl.

But again, here I was. I was putting myself in the same exact situation but I couldn't help it. Being with Jalen was wrong but it felt so damn good. He must have sensed that he went too hard on me because I watched his face soften up. Jalen ran his hands over his face as he delicately chose his next words. I could tell that this was the end of the conversation by the look of finality written all over his face. I could tell by his eyes, that he was really done with me this time. "I love you, Jeryn. I always have and always will. You got a nigga's heart. I tried to be that nigga for you, baby, but it's clear I wasn't enough and I respect that because I know I was good to you. As far as Jeidyn and this baby go, I'll be there. You already know you can count on me. But you and I are over." Then Jalen escorted me out.

I knew that my kids and I would probably be safer at Eryanna's so I stopped at a few stores to buy a few days' worth of clothes for me and my girls. There was no way that I could go back to the home I used to share with Axl. I knew that him and his goons would be everywhere, so I had no choice but to chill with my sister until I could get back into my own. The girls were so excited to see 'Auntie Ery' after I picked them up from daycare. As always, they sang loudly the entire drive there. The fact that they had no idea what was going on made me happy, but after the meeting I'd had with Jalen, all I wanted was some peace and quiet. Actually, I really wanted to lay in my bed and cry. Whether anyone believed it or not, I had love for Axl. But I wasn't in love with Axl and that was the different. Besides, that was before I found out he was the one behind my father's death. However, Jalen had hold of something that nobody else could ever claim ownership of. My heart. I had barely pulled into my sister's driveway before Jersei and Jeidyn jumped out of the car. Usually, I would've been yelling for them to be careful but I was grateful for the two seconds of peace. I grabbed the two bags out of our trunk and waddled to my sister's front door. Eryanna, who had been holding the door open for my babies, took one look at my miserable ass and started laughing.

"Damn, my niece is tearing you up." She chuckled

and without thinking, I shot her my middle finger. That only succeeding in making her laugh harder. She was lucky that I was too tired to fight her or say anything else to her. As soon as I got to her recliner, I plopped down into it and sighed. Frustration was written all over my face.

"I don't know what's going on Ery," I exclaimed, blowing a wild curl out of my face. "With Jeidyn and Jersei, I had so much energy right until the end. Remember?" I groaned, trying to get as comfortable as possible with the baby switching positions every three seconds. "I'm not even six months yet and I'm not sure how long I'm going to last. It's all too much." My sister seemed unfazed and shrugged like she wasn't even listening to me. I could tell by the look on her face that her mind was somewhere else but I didn't push it. I almost jumped out of my skin when I heard a loud banging on the door but Eryanna jumped up eagerly and then patted my knee like I was a dog.

"It's just Trill. Relax." She chuckled. When she skipped to the door like an overexcited schoolgirl, I could've sworn I felt vomit come up my throat. Though I could thank Trei, known as Trill around here, for being the person to introduce me to Jalen, I didn't think he was the man for Eryanna. Yet, she was madly in love with him. She deserved the world and I knew he couldn't be the one to give that to her. When she came back to the couch with a brown bag in her hand, I raised my eyebrows in curiosity.

"Trying to get lit huh?" I laughed, noticing how she held that bag in her hands like a newborn baby. When she pulled its contents out of the dull brown packaging though, I gasped. The moment that Eryanna nodded, I felt myself coming to tears. "Are you serious, Ery?" She nodded again and I jumped up and down, squealing, for as long as my aching body would allow me. My little sister was going to be a mommy.

"We're not for sure yet, but I think so… I'm late and you know that I'm never late. Besides, I've been really tired and nauseous lately." She explained, sighing out of aggravation. Before I could say anything else, Eryanna started to shake her head. "Trei's pull-out game sucks." When my little sister noticed the tears welling up in my eyes, she began to cry like a hungry baby.

"Ery, why are you crying? A baby is a blessing." I tried to calm her down but she was hysterical and I had a feeling that it had to do with more than just a small pregnancy scare. Eryanna looked up into my eyes and my heart nearly broke from the fear hiding in her eyes.

"Maybe for you, but what the fuck am I going to do with a baby?"

# Chapter Four:

*"Say I'm your queen. I don't want to leave this." -NIKI*

"What do you mean, Eryanna? You're going to suck it up and raise my niece or nephew. You're twenty-two fucking years old. You're not a baby. You have your own place, your own car and your own business. Any baby you give birth to will be lucky to call you mommy." I thought the speech would be exactly what she needed to hear but it only made Eryanna cry louder. When she stuck her head in my lap like she did when we were kids, I ran my fingers through her braids as she muttered incoherently.

"Trill doesn't want the baby." Eryanna cried and I rolled my eyes. Somehow that wasn't surprising to me, considering Trill already had five other kids with three different women.

"Ery, listen… If Trill chooses not to be in your baby's life, that's on him. All you can do is try your best, but I will tell you this… Your baby won't want or need for anything and I put that on my kids. You're not the first single mom out there and you definitely won't be the last. But you're sure as hell not alone. You have me and I'll do anything for you and that baby. You know that right?" Eryanna never looked up. She just nodded her head while it was still buried in my lap and that broke me. As the older sister, I was supposed to be the boulder but that had never been the case. Ery had always been the strong glue to keep our sisterhood together and now, I had no idea what to do for her. This version of Eryanna January was a new one for me. Pushing her off of me so she could get herself together, I threw the tests in her lap. "Besides, you're freaking out and we don't even know if you're pregnant yet."

Four minutes later, Eryanna stepped out of bathroom and I had my answer by the look written all over her face. She was *definitely* pregnant. I was secretly excited about my niece or nephew but Eryanna wasn't in that stage yet, so I kept my mouth shut. "Whatever you decide to do, I'm here for you." Once that was said, we got the kids to bed and watched re-runs of Martin until we laughed ourselves to sleep. The next morning, I woke up while the rest of the house was still sleeping and got ready for my doctor's appointment. I thought about asking Eryanna if she wanted to come, but I changed my mind when I saw how comfortable her and Jeidyn were, all cuddled up in her bed. Jeidyn was tucked under Eryanna since she couldn't sleep without body heat and Eryanna's arm was wrapped protectively around her. No matter what my sister thought, I knew that she was going to be a great mom. I could tell that just by the way that she loved my girls and they didn't even come out of her womb. I didn't feel like driving so I ordered an Uber and while he drove, I leaned back and rested my eyes even though it was a very quick ride. I quickly checked in once I got to my doctor's office and sat down while I waited for the nurse to call my name.

"Jeryn January!" She called as I quickly got up and looked around the room. I didn't have to worry about my enemies lurking around the maternity ward of the hospital, but in my dad's words, 'you never know who was just standing around and waiting for you to fuck up. Be on point at all times.' The nurse quickly checked me in, monitored my weight and blood pressure while I waited for my doctor. When she came in, an ultrasound technician rolled in right behind her and I found myself becoming anxious, as always, to see my little bean. It didn't matter to me that I had spent so much time being upset about having my third girl because the idea was starting to grow on me now. I even had a name picked out for my littlest princess: Jeliyah January.

"How you doing today, mama?" My doctor, an older African lady named Coko, asked as she came into the room. Huffing, I rolled my eyes.

"I'm over it. I can't wait to not be pregnant." Rubbing my stomach, I laughed because I was only partially joking. When I was a child growing up, all I wanted to do was be a mother. But that was before everything went down and now, I was a boss ass bitch and a wonderful mom. I had the best of both worlds. When I leaned back, my doctor took her time looking for the baby's heartbeat and I instantly relaxed upon hearing that soft thumping sound. I closed my eyes and thanked God, but instantly freaked out when I opened my eyes and saw a worried look on the doctor's face. She must have sensed me looking at her because when we made eye contact, she smiled reassuringly.

"It's not a big deal or anything. I just think that we may have made a little bit of a mistake." She chuckled while I sat there but I was confused on what the joke was, and why I hadn't been let in on it. She flipped the machine so that I could see exactly what it was that she was talking about and then pointed to the area right in between my baby's legs. The moment that I did, I started laughing as well. "Congratulations, Jeryn. You're finally getting your boy." Everything else checked out during my appointment so after reminding me to keep my stress levels down, my doctor sent me out of the room with a kool-aid smile on my face. Knowing I had one more stop I needed to make before I headed home, I headed towards Jalen's house. Yes, I hated him. I wanted to knock his head off. However, in order to get what I wanted, I had to keep it cool. I sped to his driveway and parked crooked, because I knew I would only be there for a second. His car was sitting in the driveway so I knew that he was home. I knocked, and then heard footsteps too light to be Jalen's come to the door. Before it even unlocked, I cursed under my breath. Sure enough, Harmony opened the door and my eyes fell out of my head when I noticed her full belly on display. I hadn't seen that at the wedding. Jalen popped up and I had the sudden urge to deck him in his jaw, but I closed my eyes and counted to ten instead. It wasn't even worth saying anything though so I just walked away. At first. But with me being me, I knew that I had to have the last word so I turned around and threw my ultrasound picture at him. It was paper so of course it did some weird fluttering shit, but I tried.

"I thought you might want to know that you're finally getting your boy." I shouted, not even looking at his face while I walked away. I wanted so badly to cuss Jalen out, but at the end of the day, I did this to myself. Jalen was right. I was selfish as fuck for expecting him not to move on and I had a whole ring on my finger. I only got about two minutes away before Jalen started blowing my phone up, back to back. I didn't even feel up to a conversation with him, so I blocked him on everything. My baby must have felt my mood change because he started moving around. That made me chuckle. I put my hand to my stomach and took a deep breath. "Don't worry, baby boy. Mommy got you. Mommy always got you."

I knew that I hadn't gone to check on the trap in a minute, so I made a quick stop. Not only that, but I had something on my mind and I needed to talk to them about it. I was pleasantly surprised to see that they had kept the place clean when I walked in, even though it had only been a few days since my last surprise pop-up. They knew about my pregnancy but I'd seemingly blew up overnight, and their eyes bulged out of my head when they saw how round I'd grown in just a few short days. My baby wasn't what I'd came to talk about though, so I sat them all down and waited until I had their attention. Clearing my throat, I prepared to be the deliverer of bad news. "Honestly, girls… I thought this third time would be a breeze just like my other two. We were under the impression that I was getting another girl but my doctor discovered today, that this lone is a boy," I explained, stopping to rub my stomach. "He's putting me through hell. I'm not able to come and go as I please any more. Hell, I can't even go up the stairs when I want. It's really starting to run my body down and not only that, but I've discovered that more than anything, I want to be around so I can be a mother to my children. This game is hard and the streets are hard. Though I was made for it, I think it's time for me to step back and focus on being there for my babies. But I would never just leave you all hanging so I'm going to be giving you twenty G's a piece. That should be enough to last you until you find your next gig, because I know you will. Also, you guys can stay here for as long as you want. The mortgage is paid off. This house can be yours." We'd become somewhat of a family so I expected them to be sad, but by the time I finished talking, a couple of them were crying like babies. I walked back into the room where my safe was and pulled all of the money out of it. Since I wouldn't be in the area like that anymore, there was no use in keeping money stashed here. That would only result in the girls being made targets. It had to be around two million dollars stashed away so I quickly divided up their cuts and then put the rest in my bag to save for a rainy day. I had been really nervous about giving up one of my main streams of income, but it had to be done at the end of the day. My daughters were starting to get older and I didn't want any bad karma to fall on them. Besides, everyone around knew what kind of business the January's were into and I didn't want them hearing about my dirty work. The streets had a funny way of talking. Besides, if I knew how to do one thing, it was to make a bag so there would be plenty of opportunities out there for me and my family. One day, I'd let everything about the game go, but that day wasn't today. When I walked out of my office, I gave each girl their portion and a hug. By the time I went down the line, I was tired and ready for a nap so I walked to the door. But just as I opened the door to leave, Kisa called my name.

"You're not just going to disappear on us, are you? You'll still come around right?" she asked. I nodded my head and the smiles on all their faces made the bittersweet pill easier to swallow.

"Of course. You girls are a part of my family."

"Good. Then come back next weekend so that we can throw you a baby shower." She suggested. I nodded again when all the other girls began to clap in agreement. I knew that if I didn't agree, they would never let me leave so I agreed and left. I was in need of some food and a nap. I walked out of the door and got in my car. Due to my pregnancy brain, I was right around the corner from Eryanna's house before I realized that I needed to deposit the rest of the money in my bag and even with how tired I was, I turned the car around and sped to my bank. The drive-thru line was too line was too long and I was in a horrible mood, so I didn't feel like talking to anyone. Regardless though, I put my big girl panties on, grabbed my bag and walked up the machine. If I had been smart about it, I would have walked into the bank but I didn't feel like being bothered with people. Quickly walking up to the deposit machine, I glanced around to check my surroundings and then put in the card for Jeidyn, first. I had enough money to make sure all our needs were met and the girls had everything they ever wanted in life, so my next mission in life was always making sure that my babies' futures were secure. I began to count my money to put it into the machine and then I heard a familiar click, along with the pressure of hard metal against the back of my head.

# Chapter Five:

*"Got this bitch rockin' like we never left." –Kash Doll*

"You do not know who you're messing with." I said loudly, secretly hoping someone would walk out of the bank and see what was happening. This wasn't the first time that I had ever had a gun held to my head, but it was the only time that I'd ever been caught slipping without my piece on me. *It would be the last time too.* My only thought was protecting my innocent unborn son.

"Give me all your money." The person demanded, trying to mask their voice but I recognized it. *I knew that person.*

"Al? Little Al?" I almost laughed because I couldn't believe Axl really had his scrawny ass little nephew trying to rob me. With anyone else, I would have pulled the razor from my boot and cut him ear to ear but I couldn't bring myself to do that to him. It wasn't his fault that he was the stupidest nigga alive to think that he could rob me and get away with it. He had me so focused on him that my guard wasn't up the way that it should have been and I didn't see the man sneaking up behind me. By the time I caught a glimpse of him out of my peripheral vision, it was too late to fight back. I saw the butt of the gun come down on me and heard a woman in the background before everything went black. I woke up a few minutes later and to my surprise, that stupid nigga didn't even manage to take any of my money. He and his accomplice were such pussies that the woman coming to help me scared him off. She quickly helped me stand to my feet while I worked hard to get my vision to focus.

"Are you alright, honey? We should call the police, Ms. January." Once my vision came all the way back, I realized the woman who had come to help me was Rae, a bank teller I'd become quite close to over the years. I quickly shook my head because I knew that there was only way to handle this and it didn't involve calling the boys. Not *those* boys, anyways. I knew I needed reinforcements other than my sister.

"No, I'm okay. Thank you for all your help," I shouted, waving her off. Once I was in my car and heading to Eryanna's house, despite Rae's argument to at least stay and get checked out, I pressed the button on the side of my Bluetooth. "Call J3."

Jerry Armani January the 3rd, aka 'J3', was my brother. He was born when my father was fourteen years old. When I was born, he was twelve years old and though he lived with his mom mostly, we got to see him as often as we could. When I was four, J3's mom remarried and moved to Dayton. My dad was crushed but we still made about three trips a year to see him when my dad wasn't busy working. When my father died, J3 and I split up our father's territories and he stayed in the mid-west to be close to his mother and his other siblings. Even though we weren't close in distance, I knew what was up. After all these years, if someone wanted smoke with me, they would have to go through him first. That was my big brother. J3 and I had always had a special connection, so he probably felt something was wrong and that's why he picked up on the second ring.

"What's wrong? I just got this weird ass feeling." Barely letting him get his sentence out, I broke down almost immediately. After explaining everything that had happened from start to finish, I had to take a moment to catch my breath and collect my thoughts. When he started to laugh, I rolled my eyes. The opposite of my serious dad, my big brother was so goofy that I knew some stupid shit was about to come out of his mouth. "So you're finally getting your boy. You done now, right?" He laughed. It figured that the only thing my brother would hear was the fact that he was finally getting his nephew. I could hear shuffling and as if he could tell that I was about to ask him what he was doing, he put me on speaker. "J, I'm about to hit my boy up to use his jet. I'll be there in a few hours so keep your phone on." He directed and I nodded as if he could see me. Then it was my turn to ask him a question.

"Speaking of babies, when you gonna have one?" His hysterical laughter asked that question for me.

"What you spend on diapers and milk, I spend on weed, bottle and bitches. I like being able to get up and go when I want and not have to worry about shit. Plus, why I gotta have one? You're the one just popping them out. I'll just borrow one of yours if I need 'em to get the ladies."

"Fuck you, J3." I said before hanging up on my brother and then laughing. J3 must have inherited some of my father's contacts after all because not even four hours later, he was calling me to let me know that he'd landed in Florida. It was late so he went ahead to his hotel to get a few hours of rest. But I couldn't sleep at all. Between my baby boy becoming a circus acrobat inside of my womb and how stupid I felt for ever trusting Axl, I tossed and turned all night. I couldn't even believe that Axl had betrayed the truce like that. He had to pay and I intended to make sure that he did.

# *Chapter Six:*



*"If you ain't gang, you ain't important."- Calboy*

"Eryanna, are you good?" J3 asked me as I forced myself to put on a fake smile for my big brother. Hell no, I definitely wasn't good. Still, I couldn't bring myself to say the two major words that I knew my brother needed to know. I was in my feelings, but at the end of the day, I needed to talk to Trill before I made any decisions. I was definitely going to make up my own mind but as the father of my child, I knew that he at least deserved to know what was going on. Not that he would care. I was stupid enough to fuck with him knowing his take on the relationship and family thing, and now I was about to be baby mama number four. Instead of telling the full-on truth, I fabricated a little.

"I miss my mom." I choked. That wasn't really a lie. I missed my mom every moment of every day but with the line of work my family and I were in, showing emotion was just a no-no. Jeryn leaned over me and gave me a half-hug, patting my back just to shut me up. I almost pushed her off me but decided to let her be. I heard her suck her teeth and I rolled my eyes. My dad had done right naming my older sister after him, because Jeryn was just like him. When our mother, Eryn, killed herself when I was fourteen years old, Jeryn and our dad shared the exact same mindset. If she was selfish enough to leave us like that, then fuck her. But I was a mama's girl all the way and when Eryn Chanel January put that bullet through her head, she took my heart with her. Secretly though, my father was self-destructing and neither my sister or I knew about it. My father's businesses, both legal and illegal, were flourishing but we didn't know he was starting to use his own product. It wasn't until our mother's autopsy report came back that everything started to make sense to us. Our father had never been a faithful man to our mom. As a matter of fact, most of the men in the January family were known as hoes. When my mother's test results came back that she was HIV positive, she ended her life rather than let that horrible disease take her. In order to cope with the grief and guilt of knowing he was the reason behind her death, our father decided to instead torment himself with a slow death. By the time that I turned seventeen, I'd lost both of my parents. Then Jeryn slowly lost her mind. She was already married to Axl at that time and had given birth to Jersei, she had started handling daddy's affairs even though J3 offered to take over everything. It seemed like our system was working, but now with Jeryn balancing two babies with another one on the way and the business, she was being caught slipping and we couldn't have that. She had no idea but I'd spoken to J3 before she had a chance to, and my big brother finally agreed with me for once. Jeryn was unintentionally starting to move messy and that wasn't good for any of us so J3 was going to take over from. My sister would finally be able to sit her ass down for once. Right when my brother was about to speak up and say something, my doorbell rang and I frowned. Nobody ever showed up at my house unannounced. As a matter of fact, only a few people even knew where I lived and the majority of them were in the room with me. The only other person was Trill and he had a key to my condo so he never needed to ring the doorbell. I got up to answer it but J3 stopped me and headed to the door instead. That's when I knew something was up. I could hear him talking to someone who sounded like a female and right when I got up, he came back in the room with a woman trudging behind him slowly. Her eyes were wide open like a doe caught in the headlights. Yet, she seemed calm and collected and held her bag in front of her like she was some kind of lawyer.

"I'm glad you have yourself a little boo, J3. But I don't think that right now is the time for introductions." I snapped, completely thrown off when they both began to laugh. Jeryn and I both shared the same confused look and that's when the young woman stepped forward and extended her hand.

"I've been waiting for this moment all my life. My dad has shown us pictures of you since I was a baby." She explained, acknowledging the curiosity written all over our faces because she continued to talk. "My name is Bellah January. You and Jeryn are my sisters."

I stuttered, searching for words as I looked to Jeryn for help but she was just as lost as me. We were both frozen but when I looked to J3, I could tell that he had already known about this. He didn't even seem surprised and barely blinked any eye while he waited for Jeryn and I to react. I ignored Bellah completely and turned to my brother. When I was younger, my brother and I had come to blows a few times so I knew that there was no way I would win. If I could have though, I would have knocked his head off.

"You knew about this, J3?" When he nodded, I felt my entire body heat up and without thinking, I swung on him. J3 hadn't been expecting it and honestly neither had I, because when my fist connected to his jaw, both of our eyes nearly fell to the ground. He grabbed my wrist and I immediately regretted my decision.

"Let that be the last time you put your hands on me. Sister or not, I don't tolerate that shit from nobody." Giving my hand a powerful, strong squeeze, I could hear the venom in his warning. When he let my hand go, I dropped it back to my side quickly. The look in his eyes scared me because it was the same look I'd seen in my father's when he would get mad. Letting it go, I turned back to Bellah.

"My dad took care of all of his kids and I've never once heard about you. What makes you think you're my sister? You don't look like us." I snipped, probably ruder than I needed to be. I felt like I was telling the truth. Jeryn, J3 and I had all inherited these high cheekbones from our father. Jeryn and I had inherited the same caramel macchiato skin as him, while our brother was a dark hazelnut color like his mother. But we all resembled each other. Bellah looked like none of us or our father. Or maybe she did and I just couldn't see it. She wasn't mad about my response. As a matter of fact, it seemed that she had been expecting it and nodded her head, reaching in her bag at the same time. Jeryn and I both stepped closer to see what it was that she was pulling out and while she looked for it, she invited herself to sit on my couch. I almost cussed her out but Jeryn saw the look on my face and put her hand on my shoulder to calm me down. Bellah never once looked up, continuing to sort and organize everything from her bag onto the table. I saw pictures, papers, letters and documents that nearly made me jaw fall to the floor. My first thought was that she was a professional con, but the more that I glanced at everything, the more it seemed to make sense. She had pictures. Everything dating back from when she was a baby to stuff that looked like it had been within the last decade, right before my dad died. There was even a picture with her, two small children and my dad what looked to be pretty close to his time of death. She saw the way I stared at that picture intently and stepped forward.

"That's our dad and my daughters, Juliana and Aaliyah," She announced proudly. I could tell that Bellah's kids had adored the hell out of our father, much like Jersei would have if she would have had more time with him. Sighing, she saw the questions in my eyes and sat down. "You didn't know about us and we didn't find out about you either until after the lawyer contacted us." One thing that I noticed was that she kept using pronouns like 'us' and 'we'. I was going to ask her what she meant, but when she looked up, she clarified and handed us another picture after hugging it close to her heart. When I saw it, my heart dropped. My father had a whole other family. In this picture, he had one arm holding a small pink bundle that I assumed was Bellah and an older boy who appeared to be about four. Looking at the time stamp in the corner, I frowned. If she was just born around the date the picture was showing, our birthdays were

only weeks apart. "That's me and my brother Jerymiah."
Hearing the name, both Jeryn and I started laughing. That
was the only thing I could do to keep from freaking out.

# *Chapter Seven:*

*"Money talk, mine speakin' the fastest." -JayDaYoungan*

I pressed my hands to my temples as I prayed that the throbbing in my head would stop. I knew one thing for certain, no matter how much my doctor disagreed and told me to relax, this shit wasn't normal. There was no way I was supposed to have a body-weakening headache that lasted this long. I couldn't keep anything down and even the smell of food made me want to bury my head in the toilet. But despite the pain and the overwhelming feeling I had to throw up, I had things to do. I was determined to get them done. I had a strange feeling that my son was going to make his grand entrance early so my first step was to do a little baby shopping. I couldn't wait to see the look on everyone's face when they found out I was actually having a boy, and not another little girl. I felt him start to move around and kick, so I rubbed my stomach and stopped to grab a bite to eat. I only took three or four bites before I felt like I was going to be sick, and threw the rest of my food away.

The moment that I pulled up into Axl's driveway,

aiming to just be in and out, I knew that something was wrong. A black car pulled in right behind me and I slapped the steering wheel, cursing under my breath. I was boxed in. When I noticed two white men get out of the car, I relaxed but only for a moment. I stayed put and only rolled my window down an inch. My piece was at my side, and I was willing and ready to use it. There was no way in hell that I was about to get ambushed again. The older white man patted on my window as if I wasn't already looking right at him and then pressed his badge against the window so that I could see it clearly.

"Mrs. Bailey-," the officer started out before I waved my hand, cutting him off completely.

"It's Ms. January." I corrected him, remaining cool on the outside. On the inside was a different story. He seemed unbothered by my comment and continued to tap on the window, making me grit my teeth. The sound of his badge hitting the glass was like nails on a chalkboard to me. "What do you need?" I asked when it was clear that he was waiting for something. His partner, a younger white man was walking around my car and I could tell that he was looking inside of it by the way he was peering around. That was a small victory, because there was nothing illegal in my car. My gun was registered in my name, so there was nothing they could do about that.

"Could you come with us, Ms. January?" he asked. When he noticed I wasn't budging, he continued to talk. "You can come with us or we can take you with us. But either way, you're under arrest." He growled at me as my eyes widened in disbelief. *This can't be happening to me.* Unlocking the car, I didn't want to put up a fight and give them any reason to shoot and kill me and my unborn son so I got out of the car. But the moment they saw I wasn't resisting or putting up a fight, both of the officers became extremely aggressive for no reason. It was like they were playing tug of war with my arms as they threw me to the ground and pinned my hands behind my back with their knee. I'd been arrested before but never like this, and never while I was pregnant.

"Please! Please stop! You're hurting me! My baby!" Since they had me face down in concrete, it was hard enough for me to breathe but the strain of one grown-ass man laying right on top of my stomach only made it worse. I was suffocating. On top of that, my head was pounding and the whole right side of my body felt like I was being stabbed. "Please! Please! I can't breathe!" I managed to beg, tears now streaming down my face and staining the concrete. Some of the neighbors came out to see what was going on and I thanked God when my next door neighbor, Mr. Allan, peered out of his window to investigate. I considered myself an introvert while we lived in that house, but we were always friendly to our neighbors and they were always friendly to us. Mr. Allan and his wife always gave the girls treats and occasionally, my daughters would go over to play with their grandkids when they were in town. I knew he would come help me.

"Jeryn, are you alright?" he yelled and I thanked God when I could hear the banging of his cane hitting the sidewalk as he made his way to me.

"Move back, sir!" the younger officer barked, but even though my head was pinned down, I could see Mr. Allan wasn't budging. I'd always thought that he had been a gangster in his younger days. He reminded me of my father in a lot of different ways. With his gun pointed right at Mr. Allan's head, I don't believe he even blinked. Even though it wasn't like I could see that far.

"Do you think your gun scares me, young man? If you're going to shoot me, shoot me! But I won't let you two manhandle that young lady! Don't you see she's pregnant?" He argued.     By this time, people had started to pull their cameras out to capture what was going on and I guess the cops got spooked. The older officer got off of me and pulled me up by my arms, while Mr. Allan continued to yell and curse at them. After cutting off my circulation to put the handcuffs on, they threw me in the back of the car and I could feel my son in there, moving around. I could tell he was giving me a sign that he was okay and since I couldn't rub my stomach, I leaned my head and thanked God.

I had a whole attitude after the cops tried to be big and bad, body-slamming me like I was a grown-ass man. But now, I had a bigger problem. For the past two hours that they had me stashed away like some prisoner, I hadn't felt my son move at all. I was sure that I needed to go to the hospital, because this just wasn't normal for my baby. My head was throbbing and in my gut, I just knew something was wrong. I could feel it. When the detective marched his way in like he was proud of the way his comrades had manhandled me, I immediately leaned over, cooling his forehead down with the cold, metal table.

"Ms. January, I'm sorry for having you wait." He snarled. His sarcasm made me want to puke and I fought not to roll my eyes.

"No you're not," I responded quickly, not in the mood for whatever foolishness he was about to bring my way. "What is it that you have me in here for? I want my lawyer. Call my lawyer." I demanded. The entire room was now spinning and before I knew it, I was rushing to the garbage can to empty my stomach contents into it. The officer was completely repulsed and stood back in disgust while I gagged. When I finished, he handed me a napkin and a bottle of water, which I had a problem handling considering I was still in handcuffs. I closed my eyes until my stomach stopped turning and when I was sure that I was good, I opened my eyes to stare down the detective, who was clearly lost about what to do from here. "I want my lawyer." I repeated again, just in case he didn't hear me the first time. I had a strange pain in my left arm, but shook it off to being slammed like a thief.

# Chapter Eight:

*"I never fold, never bend."*- 03 Greedo

After freeing myself from Trill's embrace for the millionth time to go pee, I came back to bed and couldn't find a comfortable position to lay in. Even with Trill's strong arms engulfing me, I felt uneasy about something. At about three o'clock in the morning, right when I had managed to close my eyes and drift back off to sleep, my phone started ringing off the hook and I just knew something was up. Jeryn knew better than to call me at this time of night unless it was an emergency. I didn't talk to anybody but Jesus until at least 11 am. When I glanced at the screen and saw our family's attorney calling me, I panicked.

"Hello?" I croaked, my voice still full of sleep. I shifted to sit up so that I could avoid waking up Trill as I walked into the living room.

"Hi, Ms. January. I'm calling because I just received a call from Jeryn. She just called us from the police station. Do you want to meet us there so you can drive her home? I don't suspect we'll be there long." the lawyer asked as my heart started palpitating.

"Wait, police station? Hold on," I covered the phone with my hand while I went back into the bedroom to try and shake Trill awake. "Baby, wake up. They arrested Jeryn. We gotta go to the police station." I was expecting  him to be groggy because he had been out making plays with Jalen all night, but hearing that my sister was in jail caused him to spring up instantly like a loose cannon. As he walked away, going to put on some clothes in the bathroom and calling someone I assumed was Jalen, I got back on the phone with the lawyer. "We'll be right there. Where are my nieces?"

"From my understanding, they are at the police station as well. In case the stay is overnight, you'll need to sign for them to be released into your care." That's all I needed to hear so I hung up the phone and quickly got my shoes on. Trill was already at the door with his keys in hand and he was off the phone, ready to go. That surprised me, because him and my sister were hardly ever on good terms. As we drove, sped actually, to the police station, he held my hand in reassurance the entire way. I was glad that he was starting to understand that my sister was one of the most important people in my life to me. Niggas were temporary but my family was forever, so my sister was my biggest priority. Sparing me a few smiles along the way, Trill even managed to rub my stomach a few times. The small pudge wasn't huge but I could tell that something was there and obviously, he could too. I could only imagine what he felt knowing that his sixth child was on the way, but this was my first and honestly, I was excited, but confused on what would become my future. At least Trill knew what to expect. Just as I was about to get lost in the thoughts of what our child would look like, and if we would have a boy or a girl, Trill pulled up and I barely gave him time to park before I hopped out of the car and walked inside the building. Usually, so many niggas with guns would freak me out but my father had taught us how to present ourselves in public so I sat down and waited patiently for our lawyer to show up. I wasn't speaking to anyone until he got there. That's why we paid him as much as we did. So he could speak for us. As we waited, it was my turn to reassure Trill. He was clearly shook about being surrounded by cops so I rubbed his leg. We both sighed in relief when the lawyer walked through the door and headed straight to us. But I could tell something was up by the look on his face so I stood up to greet him and shook his hand firmly, staring him straight in the eyes like my father had taught me. That's how you get a nigga to take you serious. I skipped all the formalities of introducing Trill to my lawyer and immediately began asking questions. Actually, I asked the only question I could think of at the moment.

"What are they saying? What's wrong?" I panicked and mentally prepared myself for the worst because the look on my lawyer's told me everything I needed to know. Whatever he was about to say, wasn't good.

"Ms. January, I'm going to be honest with you. They have a strand of your sister's hair at the scene of a crime. The scene where a young, pregnant woman was killed…" I was glad that the lawyer was being honest, but that didn't help cure my confusion. Jeryn wasn't a killer by any means, though we sometimes did what we had to do. But I knew Jeryn like the back of my hand. She definitely wasn't about to kill a pregnant woman. We didn't do those kinds of things, because karma sometimes had a way of coming back and making you choke. Besides, our dad had taught us the original code of the streets. Women and children were off limits. Not to mention, my sister and I talked about everything. She had never told me anything about that.

"A woman? Who?"

"Officially, I can't tell you because her family hasn't released permission for her to be identified publicly yet. But unofficially, her name is Harmony Hicks, known around as Money. She's the wife of Jalen Hicks, your sister's ex-lover." That fact alone let me know that while the cops may have something on my sister, they were just theorizing, talking to hear themselves talk. There was nothing 'ex' about Jeryn and Jalen. On and off like a light switch, I was just waiting for them to stop playing games and realize they were made for each other. Jalen didn't need Harmony and Jeryn didn't need Axl. They needed each other, but they were too stubborn to accept it.

"When was this?" I asked, my heart now pounding in my throat. I knew Jeryn and she wasn't capable of something like this, but I couldn't lie and say the thought didn't cross my mind that she had done it. After all, she was crazy in love with Jalen. Plus she was just crazy anyways. That was a bad combination. But when the lawyer told me the date they suspected Harmony was murdered, I frowned and checked my phone. My memory had started to suck over the past few months so I put everything in my phone. That's how I knew that something didn't sound right. I showed him everything, which included the fact that Jeryn was with me and J3 all night, and watched as a glimmer of hope flashed in his eyes. That was all I needed to see, so I continued to search through my phone in hopes of finding something that would free my sister. That's when I got an idea and repeated a number to him, over and over again until I was sure that he had itput in his phone. "That's the number to the leasing agent in my building. Every visitor that comes into the building is required to check in. My sister was with my brother and I, our other sister, and the kids all night long. Call them. They'll confirm it and give you access to the surveillance cameras. She didn't even leave my house until 1 P.M. That was to go baby shopping. " I spoke matter of factly. He quickly wrote everything down that I was saying and then walked over to a cop while I held my breath in anticipation.

"Jonte Carter. Ms. January's lawyer. May I have a private moment with my client please?" he demanded as I folded my hands in solidarity. The police could give me all the dirty looks they wanted to. If I didn't hear from my sister and make sure she was okay, I wasn't going anywhere. After they allowed him access to Jeryn and shut the door right behind him, I walked up to the glass and immediately my stomach dropped to my knees. Something was wrong with my sister. Jeryn was clammy and sweaty. All of the color had left her body and though she was nodding her head weakly to respond to the lawyer's questions, I could tell that she wasn't all the way there.

"What's wrong with her? What's wrong with my sister? What did you guys do to her?" I asked, facing a cop who chose to ignore me. Stepping right in front of him, I made it so that he had no choice but to acknowledge me. "I know you hearing me talking to you and I promise you, if you keep ignoring me and something happens to my sister, your ass is mine. This whole department's ass is mine. What's wrong with her?" I asked again, yelling this time just to get my point across. I must have been too in his face because he slightly pushed me back, and I lost my balance. That's when Trill got involved.

"I don't give a fuck about that badge you're wearing homie. Don't touch that one." He warned the cop, stepping extremely close to me. Though it felt good to know I was protected, Trill's involvement now had me on edge. With one wrong move from the cop, Trill could turn this shit into a riot real quick and I didn't need that right now. I just needed to know my sister was alright. The officer seemed to not want any issues with us and backed away, but that didn't solve my problem. Something was wrong with Jeryn. It was written all over her face. Nobody was doing anything about it so I did the next best thing that I could think of. I began to yell and bang on the window, so that Jeryn could hear me.

"Jeryn, it's okay! I'ma get you out! I promise! You'll be home soon! I got you!" The distraction was loud enough to get the attention of other cops around me and they did their best to remove me from the room, but I wasn't going out like that. About my sister, it was going to be war. When she heard my voice, Jeryn tried to stand up but was holding onto the edge of the table for support. When I saw her eyes roll into the back of her head, I tried to rush into the room but the officers held me back. Then out of nowhere, Jeryn collapsed out onto the ground. The officers could try to keep me out of the station but I knew my rights and I wasn't leaving until the ambulance did. I sat in the car with Trill holding my hand and waited for the ambulance to arrive while I formulated a plan. Since they wouldn't allow me to talk to my sister, I was just going to have to go around them. When I watched Jeryn being loaded up into the ambulance on a gurney, I asked Trill to follow behind at a safe distance. I knew how the system worked, but they weren't going to get my sister like that. Not as long as I had breath in my body. On the way there, I called J3 who did his best to calm me down but I was starting to become hysterical. Jeryn had never even had the flu and now that she was pregnant, seeing her helpless like that had me feeling weak. After he assured me that he was on the way to the hospital to meet us, I hung up as I did my best to relax and trust that Jeryn would be just fine. My hands were shaking the entire time but thankfully, we made it there right after the ambulance. When I saw the doors opening and them performing CPR on her as they attempted to stabilize her, I lost every bit of calmness that I'd had before. I was crying, screaming and Trill had to hold me back as I tried to fight my way to my big sister. The nurses only let us get to a certain point so when they banned me from going back in the room with her, the only thing that I could do was plead for someone to please save her life. If I lost Jeryn, I had no idea what I'd do. When I finally managed to run out of tears, Trill held my hand as I watched aimlessly at how many times the little hand went around the clock. Before I knew it, hours had passed. I paced. I prayed. At one point in time during that night, I actually swore that I was going crazy for a moment. I became so bored that I tried to distract myself with scrolling through my social media, but all I ended up doing each time was looking at pictures of Jeryn and I. Us at our mother's funeral, us at our father's funeral and then just random pictures of Jeryn and the girls. Just as I was about to start getting rowdy and begging someone for an update, J3 stormed in and I rolled my eyes when I saw Bellah following closely behind him. I shut up because Jeryn was way too important to be starting petty drama while I waited for some type of news. Besides, Trill gave me a look that told me to act my age. Paternity drama that really had nothing to do with me wasn't even worth it. Not right now, at least. I guess my face must have said everything without me needing to, because J3 said nothing to me as he sat down and waited with us. Instead, he just squeezed my shoulder and since my big brother wasn't the most affectionate person around, I'd take what I could get when it came to J3. He must have been my good luck charm though because the moment that he sat down, a doctor came out and stormed right towards us. I stood up and held J3's hand anxiously in one hand and Trill's in the other. I was praying for some good news but preparing for the worst of it.

"The family of Jeryn January, correct?" he asked.

"I'm her sister." I announced, side-eyeing Bellah as she began to cough awkwardly. I could tell that she was trying to make a point, but I ignored her.

"We're her sisters." She emphasized, only making me roll my eyes harder. I glared at her waiting for her to say something else. But she wasn't stupid. I was close enough to reach over and slap her. She seemed unfazed and stared right back at me until the doctor interrupted our moment.

"Well, we were able to save your sister. Jeryn suffered a stroke," he explained, stopping me in my tracks right when I was about to start asking questions. "I know your sister was young, Ms. January. Please let me explain. During pregnancy, blood flow can become impaired and your sister developed a large clot that went unnoticed. We had to perform an emergency cesarean section." My eyes nearly bugged out of my head once I realized how serious this was.

"And my niece? How is she?" I asked, panicking. Once I saw a smile appear on the doctor's face, I got a small glimmer of hope. J3 started to laugh as well so I stood around awkwardly, waiting for someone to fill me in on the joke. It was clear he knew something I didn't.

"Well Ms. January, the bad news is that your sister's gynecologist should definitely be fired. So should the ultrasound technician. Not only is your nephew unexpectedly well, but Jeryn's due date was extremely wrong. Her paperwork shows that she was almost 21 weeks pregnant, but my gestational assessment of your nephew tells me that he's at least 26 ½ weeks. He's two pounds and seven ounces in weight, and is over sixteen inches long. He's small but he's strong-willed and he's definitely a fighter. He's breathing with a little assistance, but his eyes are open. I won't say this on record, but your nephew has a very high chance of survival. Jeryn is recovering but she likely won't be awake until the morning. You can visit with her but only for a little while. She needs rest." He explained, walking away before we could ask anything else. A nurse came up behind and escorted us all to Jeryn's room. I noticed the officers outside of her room, but didn't say anything as I rushed past them. The only thing that mattered was seeing Jeryn. I felt my legs give out from under me seeing her hooked up to all of those machines like that. I didn't know what to say or do so I just pulled up a chair beside her. The doctor could say what he wanted to say but until my sister opened her eyes, I wasn't going anywhere. I had to make sure she was okay. When I tried to take her by the hand and realized that she was handcuffed to the bed, it took everything in me not to burn the hospital down. Instead, I just closed my eyes and prayed. Tears fell and I still kept my eyes closed. I almost fell asleep talking to God, but then I heard footsteps trampling in the hallway and people yelling. I looked up to see Jalen standing in the doorway. Panic was written all over his face. The marriage certificate didn't mean shit to me, and clearly Harmony didn't either when it came to Jalen and Jeryn. He was in love with my sister.

"What the fuck! What happened?" He cursed, running to Jeryn's side. Cradling her stomach in his hands, he dropped his head to her side and started to cry. I knew a lot of people believed Axl was the father of Jeryn's baby, but my sister had told me the truth. Apparently, she had told Jalen too because the worry was written all over his face. Sticking his head out into the hallway, he flagged down the first nurse that he saw, without even giving me a chance to update him on everything. "My baby, is she alright? Can I see my daughter?" he stammered, not even bothering to pause so that I could tell him he was the father of a beautiful baby boy, not a girl. The nurse seemed confused and peered into the room.

"If you're talking about Baby January, it's a boy. Not a girl." She responded rudely as he glanced at me in confusion, but then quickly turned his attention back to the nurse.

"I don't know what the fuck you're talking about. It's not Baby January. It's Baby Hicks. Can I see him? That's my son." Instinctively, I followed behind Jalen as the nurse directed him towards my nephew's room. She glanced back at me skeptically but the look on my face must have told her not to try it, because she didn't dare utter a word my way.

"Please make sure all phones are on silent or vibrate. Wash your hands then put on gloves. He's very sensitive and not quite ready for one-on-one time yet. The most you'll be able to do is stroke his hand for right now. He can hear you but his ears are extremely sensitive so speak softly." She instructed, opening the door of the room as I turned my phone off and tossed it into my purse. I never in a million years expected to see what I saw. I had no idea what a two pound baby looked like until that moment and it took everything in me not to cry. He was so small that he could fit into the palm of my hand and probably still have some space left. I did my best to calm my emotions as a quiet sob escaped my lips. The nurse sent me a warning glance and Trill, who I hadn't even realized was right behind me, snaked his arm around my waist.

"Calm down, Ery. You got this. Our nephew needs

you." He whispered in my ear as I took a deep breath to calm myself down. Jalen clearly couldn't handle the pressure of what we were seeing because he lasted all of four minutes before he exited out of the room. Trill left right behind him to make sure that he was alright. That left me and the nurse alone, which was perfect. It granted me the time to ask some important questions. I needed to know what we were up against.

"He's going to make it, right?" I questioned, honestly. She sighed sympathetically and began to break it all down for me.

"His chances are very good. His vitals look good, he's stable. I can't say for sure, but what I can say is that you should enjoy every single moment that you get with Baby January-,"

"Drayven." I corrected her.

"Excuse me?"

"Jeryn always said her first son's name would be Drayven. That's his name. It's not Baby January. His name is Drayven." Sending a soft smile my way, she wrote the name down on a piece of paper after I spelled it out for her and then stuck it to his incubator. So excited to see him, I quickly washed my hands and put on gloves as I reached in to stroke his little hand and admire how beautiful he was. That's when he grabbed me by the finger and opened his eyes, shocking the hell out of me. My nephew had the brightest, most alert gray eyes that I'd ever seen and even though he was born early, he still had a head full of jet black ringlets. That amazed me. "I love you Drayven and I got your back. You hear me? Auntie Ery got your back until forever. Mommy is going to get better. I promise you. Just watch." I whispered to him. Trill must have just been in the back just watching me, because I hadn't even noticed that he was back in the room until he stepped forward and wrapped both arms around me from behind.

"Dray Dray, Uncle Trill got y'all too. All of y'all." When he cradled my stomach in his hands, it was hard to ignore exactly what he was saying. I rubbed my stomach, the idea of being someone's mother finally starting to sink in. Trill left me to do my auntie thing and I spent twenty minutes with my nephew, singing him songs and telling him stories of all the wreckless shit me and his mommy did when we were little. Once I got hungry and felt the need for a nap, I said my goodbyes and gave my number to the nurse so they could call me with updates, or if anything changed. J3, being a bachelor, was too shook to go into the baby's room so he waited outside for us. Bellah stayed with him, which I was thankful for. When they saw me walking towards them, I prepared for them to hound me with questions.

"How is he? Is he alright?" J3 asked. I nodded and in that moment, I knew I couldn't tell them the real possibility of Drayven not making it. He was a January and that meant that he was a fighter. I knew that he would be okay and J3 needed to know that too. With him now being the head of the January Cartel entirely, it was important that he kept his head on straight.

"He's going to be fine. He looks great." I partially lied. My nephew was the cutest baby in the world to me. Giving my older brother a half-hug, the only type of affection a real nigga like him would accept, I sent a casual nod Bellah's way while she practically waited for me to acknowledge her. Trill grabbed my hand and we walked into the lobby. I felt so bad for Jalen. He was in the lobby, with his head cradled in his hands, rocking back and forth like a mental patient. Jalen didn't even care that people were watching him and he was so caught up in his grief that he hadn't even noticed us walk up to him. I knew it looked bad with all of the tubes and wires sticking out of the baby like that, but I truly believed that Jalen felt guilty; as he should. Instead of rolling my eyes and walking away like I wanted to, I decided to sit next to him and offer him a shoulder to cry on. Now wasn't the time for Jalen to lose his mind. Not when my niece and my nephew still needed their father. "Come on, J. Everything is going to be alright. You just need to pull it together. " I scolded him as if he were my child. "This isn't your fault." I partially lied. Though maybe all of this wasn't his fault, I did truly believe that Jalen held some accountability in what happened to Jeryn. I didn't doubt that he loved that Harmony chick, whoever the fuck she was, but that wasn't the reason he married her and I didn't like that. Jalen and Jeryn had some sort of sick obsession with eachother, and everything was about revenge with the two of them. Jalen married Harmony to get back at Jeryn, even though he knew if he just hung in there, Jeryn was going to file for divorce. She was just waiting for six more short weeks until he finalized a major deal. That way, half of that $5.4 million dollars would be hers.

When Jalen looked up at me, heartbreak written all over his face, I lost it. I held his head close to me while we both cried together. "I promise you… everything is going to be alright." I assured him, lying again. This time, I felt bad because I wasn't sure if what I was saying was true. I had no idea what was going to happen. I had never been this uncertain in my life before, but I no longer knew about anything. Jalen immediately stopped crying and looked me in my eyes again.

"You're right, Eryanna… and you wanna know why? I'm going to get my shit together and I'm going to marry your sister. That's where my heart is. Plus, I gotta get my babies' last names changed. The nurses in this bitch got me fucked up calling my firstborn son Baby January. Hell nah." Seeing that Jalen finally had that spark back in his eyes, I couldn't help but to laugh and quickly pushed him off of me.

"Good, now bye. I like you but I don't like you like that."

Both my sister and nephew were alive and that was what mattered to me. Eventually, he calmed himself down and so we all parted ways. Bellah went to grab her kids and J3 went to go ahead and check on the traps. I, on the other hand, wasn't leaving Jeryn's side. As I headed back to her room, I heard what sounded like a single gunshot outside of the hospital and everyone else around me must have heard it too. The hospital immediately became a crazy madhouse, with everyone running and screaming. I nearly got pushed over by people trying to get out of the way. Though I wanted to go to Jeryn's side, something told me to go make sure that Trill and Jalen were alright, but it was no use. The hospital was on lockdown with nobody going in or out. They were trying to control the scene and censor what people could see from the inside as they crowded the door, but I was determined to figure out what was going on as I pushed my way through the large group of people. Seeing the body that they were now covering up with a white sheet, I gasped and tears sped to my eyes without my permission. My worst fear was confirmed as I made eye contact with Trill, who dropped his head in defeat while he cried. Police swarmed the parking lot and the nurses soon shuffled us all away so that the police could begin their investigation. Everyone continued on with their daily lives and I was just stuck there, processing how to explain to Jeryn that Jalen was dead, or how to tell my niece that her father, the man she adored was gone. The first step though was getting Jeryn to wake up.

# Chapter Nine:

*"My youngins, they be on that gang shit." –Lil Tjay*

I watched in anticipation as Jeryn's body hit the ground at the station. Even with her ghetto ass sister in the background going off, I was enjoying the scene in front of me. Once they called me to inform me that Jeidyn and Jersei were at the police station, and I realized Jeryn was there, I quickly accepted the invitation to come retrieve my girls. Actually, my daughter and her sister. See, the thing is Jeryn thought I was stupid but I was from it. I had strong genes and Jeidyn looked nothing like me, which was an instant giveaway that she wasn't mine. My main concern was Jersey. Nothing, and nobody, mattered besides her.

I wasn't sure what happened to Jeryn, and frankly I didn't care. I left after the ambulance came. It was bittersweet because there was nothing better than watching the life slip out of the woman who had ruined my life, but I was upset that it wasn't me who was doing it. By the time that the ambulance was taking her away, I was loading the kids in the car. I wanted to see this bad but taking the girls to the hospital wouldn't allow me to move in silence like I needed to. I called my mom as I pulled up to her house and had to thank God when she was already standing out on the porch. I didn't bother to say a word as I grabbed both of the girls by the wrist and spoke to my mother. She already knew the deal and let both of them in the house as I went to go see what was going on with Jeryn. Not because I cared, but I needed to make sure the bitch was dead. As I got in my car, my mother called my name.

"Axl!" she called out, ashing her cigarette as she threw it into the bushes. To be worth so much money, she could be so ghetto sometimes. She drove me crazy, acting like she was still in the hood. When I turned around to face her, she was lighting up another cigarette. "Can you bring some money by for Azayo later?" Without going into further details, I nodded as I got back into my car and drove off.

At the hospital, it was easy to find Eryanna so I wandered for about an hour, circling around her and watching her lose her mind. She was so busy watching the clock and checking her phone that she didn't even notice me lurking around. *God, I hate that bitch.* She had been a thorn in my side since the moment Jeryn and I got involved with eachother, and she couldn't keep her nose out of my business if it meant saving her life. Had she never said anything, Jeryn would have never found out that I was messing with Money and would have never started messing with Jalen to get back at me. That would have saved me the embarrassment of everyone around me knowing that I was raising another nigga's child. All that was about to be over though, and then I could get back to doing what I was doing before all this family shit. Of course Jersei would still be taken care of, that was my baby for sure, but Jeidyn would need to be handled before I went any further.

J3 and a woman I recognized as my homeboy's baby mama were with Eryanna and her pussy ass boyfriend was there too. When the doctor came to talk to Eryanna, I observed from the shadows to make sure that I was close enough and could hear what the doctor was saying. Disappointing the fuck out of me, I did my best not to cuss out loud when I heard him say that she wasn't dead and would recover well, but I knew that I could fix that. I waited in the hallway of the nursery, pretending to look at all of the babies. In reality, I was just buying myself time. I saw Jalen run into the hospital and quickly guided myself to Jeryn's room by following him. It took everything in me not to shoot him right then and there. For over an hour, I paced back and forth and then the opportunity I was waiting for, was granted to me. Eryanna and everyone else were led to a different part of the hospital so I quickly found Jeryn's room and slipped in. I moved over to the side of her bed so that it would look like I was just praying over a close friend, but I was really trying to unplug Jeryn's breathing machine. She looked so peaceful and angelic just laying there, but I knew she would look better to me if she was dead. When I heard the door start to open, I almost tripped when I tried to move away from the plugs but the nurse entered in, skeptically peeking in like she had already saw what I was doing. I didn't want to seem suspicious but I also didn't want her to be able to recognize me, so I dipped out as quickly as I could. She tried yelling behind me but by the time security got involved, I was out of there. As I made my way to my car stored in the back corner of the parking lot, I could hear Jalen on the phone, yelling for someone to find his daughter. I could nothing but laugh as I hit the gas. I had barely made it to the street when I heard a single gunshot and then police cars came rushing past me. I didn't know what happened but I knew it wasn't good and I didn't fuck with the police, so I wasn't going to investigate.

Besides, I had something better to do and that was to handle Jeidyn. I hated that little girl and I wouldn't be able to relax with her being around. With Jeryn being alive still, the kids were just in the way of my plan so I called my boy to help me out. Once I had the kids out the way, Jeryn would be so weak she'd have no choice but to do as I said. He had no idea what we were doing because if I had told Carlo, he wouldn't have agreed to it. But this was the only way. Picking up the girls from my mom's, we got back in the car as fast as I could get them buckled in and then I pulled up on my boy. Without any questions, he hopped in and we took off. He didn't ask anything until I had him turn and stop in the middle of an abandoned road. Hopping out, I pulled Jeidyn out and then paused when Jersey unbuckled her seatbelt as well.

"Daddy will be back for you sweetheart. Just wait for me, okay?" I said softly. Then, I turned to Carlo, my homeboy, who had now jumped in the driver's seat. "Drive down to the end of the road and wait for me there." I ordered, turning with Jeidyn's hand in my own before he could ask me anything else. The less questions, the better. When I was sure that he was out of sight, I lead Jeidyn into a wooded area. "Go pick that flower for me, Jei." I said softly, watching as she ran away before I gathered up the biggest rock that I could find and held it in my hand as it began to weigh a million pounds. I wanted to do this before the three-year old could turn back around and look at me so I ran up to her and hit her once with the large object. I was expecting to have to hit her repeatedly but it seemed that it only took one time. Just to make sure though, I struck her with the rock one more time. Her body wriggled and jumped momentarily, but then it stopped and I was satisfied that Jeidyn would no longer be a problem. Strangely enough, I couldn't wipe away the smile that laid on my face and I didn't try as I walked back to the car where Carlo was waiting nervously. Upon seeing Jeidyn was no longer with me, I could tell that he knew something was up, but he still said nothing. Nobody said anything as we drove, until I stopped him to run across the street and use a pay phone. Dialing the three numbers I would never use under any other circumstances, I waited for the operator to pick up before I began to talk, hoping to convince someone of my lies.

"I need help. My daughter, Jeidyn Bailey, she's three and she's gone missing." After I said those words, I hung up the phone and got back into the car with Carlo. We got halfway down the street before Jersei tugged on my shirt.

"Daddy, where's Jei?" I couldn't even answer my daughter. The only thing I could do was stare at my hands that were now stained with her crimson blood.

# Chapter Ten:

*"'Cause what if I never love again?" –Adele*

The police were very considerate and gave us almost a week to process everything. Unfortunately, due to the fact that Trill and I were the last people to see Jalen alive, and since Trill was the closest person to Jalen, the police asked us to come down to the station to make an official statement. I wasn't sure what we were officially stating but I agreed to go- just to get them off my back. Trill, on the other hand, cussed every officer he saw from here to China. I didn't bother to try and calm him down because he'd just seen his best friend's brains splattered all over the hospital's sidewalk. Trill was allowed to feel the way he wanted, and I had no intention of stopping him. Everyone tended to grieve differently. However, I knew that just because of my last name, the police would be on me. There was no way they would leave Jeryn alone if I didn't do what they wanted me to. Besides, I had nothing to hide, especially when it came to Jalen's murder. He was like a brother to me too, so anything that I could do to help, I would.

I sat in the interrogation room, sipping on a Sprite as I tapped my acrylic nails on the table impatiently and tried to calm my flopping stomach. I couldn't believe that they had the nerve to call me here and then have me waiting for over an hour, just for someone to come and talk to me about some shit I didn't even see. Right when I was about to head out because they had no reason to keep me, an older female detective came and sat down right in front of me. Usually, I felt like they all just waited to sit around and point the finger at someone. But this detective didn't strike me like that. As a matter of fact, she seemed to be downright concerned about something and she wasn't saying anything. Not at first, anyways.

"Ms. January, thank you so much for coming in and answering some questions. I know this must be a really inconvenient time with your niece and everything,-" Her statement caught me off guard so I held up my hand to pause her in her tracks. I wasn't about to say shit until she told me what she was talking about.

"My niece? What's going on with my niece? What are you talking about?" I didn't give her a chance to answer one question before I shot out one after the other and before I could help myself, I was calling Trill while she explained to me what was happening. Standing up, I ran my hand over my face as I waited for my man to answer the phone. I was trying to listen to the detective update me at the same time.

"It seems that your brother in law-,"

"He's my soon to be ex-brother in law. They're estranged." I corrected, shooting her a glare before she could say anything else stupid. I could tell that she was tired of me cutting her off, but I didn't give a fuck.

"Well, whatever his relation to you… He has reported his daughter, your three-year old niece Jeidyn, missing. Allegedly, his car was stolen with her in it." Hearing her words, my mouth dropped. A lot of people didn't know that Jeidyn wasn't Axl's daughter but I did, and I also knew how Axl got when he became vengeful. I made a promise to myself that if he laid a finger to one strand of my niece's hair, we were going to have a problem that he wasn't ready for. I could tell that by the look on the detective's face that there was more she needed to say. She was just reluctant to tell it to me. Rather than being patient, I could feel myself about to snap but I didn't want to do that here. Especially not while Trill wasn't here. Just as I was getting ready to pop off and make a scene, I could hear a bunch of the officers' radios going off at one time.

"Young girl who appears to resemble missing girl, found! We repeat, it appears we have found the missing girl!" Hearing that, I was out of the door before anyone else could say anything and surprisingly, none of the officers asked questions. I would have cussed them out if they did. A couple of them even nodded at me, giving me permission to ride along and go get my niece. That was good and easy though, because I was going to anyways and I would have dared someone to try and stop me. The entire ride, I prayed to God that Jeidyn was unharmed, while praying that Axl was unharmed as well. Now, it was just a matter of watching him die. No matter what he had reported, I knew the truth. Jeryn always told me that Axl never knew Jeidyn wasn't his, but I didn't believe it. I could tell by the way that he looked at her, and how different he treated her from Jersei, that he knew the truth. Now, he had hurt my niece just to get her out of the way. Seeing the wooded area where they said my niece was discovered, I stood back and watched as they extracted a small, almost lifeless body out of a pile of brush.

"Jei!" I screamed, not waiting for her to be brought to me as I tripped and stumbled over branches and tree rubble, just trying to get to her. I recognized the sparkly silver shoes she was wearing and the white bow in her hair, which was now stained in crimson red blood and mud. That was my niece. Officers tried to hold me back but it was no use. About my family, all bets were off. While the paramedics worked on her, I tried my hardest not to cry my eyes out at the blood surrounding my little niece's head. I had always had my doubts about Axl, but this only confirmed the fact that he was one sick son of a bitch. I jumped up, shouting and praising God when they confirmed they had a pulse, even though it was a weak one. When they loaded her up into the ambulance, I got in too. The only thing I could do was sing her favorite song while I held her hand. A few times, I swore that I saw her eyes move but that could've just been my imagination. After being in the hospital for God knows how long, I wasn't sure what was real or fake any more. All I knew was that my sister, my niece and my nephew all needed me, and I intended to be here for them. I wasn't sure how, but I would figure it out.

I thought it was nerve wrecking waiting for news about Jeryn, but I hadn't even seen the half of it. Waiting for news about Jeidyn was a thousand times worse and yet, that's all I could do. So I waited. When I was starting to go crazy and just as my phone died, Trill ran into the hospital and took me into his arms, holding me and rocking me as I sobbed. Though I knew I would have to be strong again, being able to be vulnerable just for a moment, really felt good. We hugged until I felt intoxicated by his cologne and just as I pulled away, the doctor was coming up to us. I felt like I'd been at the hospital so much, they automatically knew who to look for. Unlike when I was being updated on Jeryn, this time when the doctor walked up to us, I had no hope. Then he smiled at me.

"Ms. January, I have good news. Though your niece has a severe concussion, there appears to be no swelling of her brain. We'd like to keep overnight for a few days just to observe her and make sure she doesn't have a brain bleed, but she should recover and be just fine. She'll be back to the Jeidyn you know in no time." He assured me before patting my back and walking off. For once, the good news was actually good and I found myself jumping around like a crazy lady. I couldn't help it. If this was the one victory God would offer me, I would take it.

Almost two weeks after that and I could say without a doubt in my mind, that was one of the small victories that God granted me and my family. Jeryn still hadn't woken up, so most of my days were spent just watching her. But Drayven was progressing nicely and doctors felt like he would be able to come home within the next couple of weeks. Jeidyn had a couple of setbacks but she was finally getting ready to come home to a house where her mother and her brother wouldn't be for a little while. I knew that God gave his toughest battles to his strongest soldiers and that meant I was doing the right thing. But it was tough, juggling and running between three different hospital rooms and still managing to eat and take care of myself. Luckily, Trill had been by my side every step of the way. J3 had to leave for a couple of weeks so he could handle business, but Bellah stopped by a few times to make sure everything was alright with us. I appreciated her making an effort. But just by constantly having to be at the hospital, I didn't have much energy to even try and entertain her. Most of the time we were together, our time was spent scrolling through our newsfeeds silently or laughing at some stupid joke on the internet. It sounded stupid, but those were the moments that I was starting to enjoy the most.

More importantly, all the time in the hospital made me think about how I would hurt Axl. He had caused too much pain in my family for me to just let it go now. It was time for him to pay. Since J3 was coming back into town and him and Bellah were coming by to handle things at the hospital so that I could shower and go spend a little time at home with my man, even though I had no intention of going home at all. As a matter of fact, I'd had it in my mind to go see Axl to get some answers, and that's exactly what I was going to do. Trill had some business to tend to, so lying to him wouldn't be an issue. He was on a money move right now, so I was his last concern. As far as Trill was concerned, I was still at the hospital. I'd be home by the time he got there. Driving to Axl's parents' house, I cursed when I noticed that neither of the cars were there but that was okay. I would just sit around and wait until they returned. I had planned on just being patient until Mr. and Mrs. Bailey came home but then I saw movement behind their curtains and decided to try my luck with whoever was there. I only had to make it to the front step before I realized Azayo, Axl's youngest brother, was the only one home. That alone caused me to smile.

Once I checked and made sure that my gun was tucked into my waistband, I rang the doorbell and tapped my foot as I heard Azayo's annoying singing come closer to the door. I smiled, but only because I was about to get vengeance for my entire family and everyone who had wronged us. I would start with the Bailey Family.

"What's up, Eryanna?" he greeted, looking me up and down. I blushed and laughed flirtatiously, but I didn't take that young boy serious. He was eighteen years old and the spitting image of Axl, so he was definitely very handsome. But he was too young and too corny for me. Besides, nobody compared to Trill in any way.

"Did we leave Jersei's ballet shoes over here? I can't find them anywhere." I asked, peering in as if I were actually looking for something. Jersei didn't even dance ballet. He walked around, looking for the imaginary pair of shoes. That's when I did it. With his back turned to me, I pointed my gun at him and pulled the trigger once. I had never missed a shot and this time was no different. As a matter of fact, it was a bullseye, hitting him dead in the middle of the back of his head. He staggered for a second but I watched as he basically fell over like the London Bridge. Blood poured from his skull and I took that opportunity to dash out of the house. I knew that with the neighborhood that they lived in, a gunshot would be reported in a half of a second. That meant I only had a little time to make my escape. Getting in my car, I took off down the opposite street since I knew not many people would go that way and it wouldn't be backed up. When I was certain that I was a safe distance away, I pulled over to a bridge and tossed my gun. I thought about tossing the black sweatshirt I had been wearing too, but I didn't have a shirt on under it. Then I drove home and took a long hot shower. I had to make sure I scrubbed myself as best as I could. Once I was satisfied that I was clean enough, I slid on a bra and a pair of panties and then slipped into bed. Not even 45 minutes later, Trill came home and joined me in bed. I feigned sleep and when he pulled me in to him, I snuggled closer like usual. Ever since I'd known him, Trill had an obsession with smelling me. Tonight was no different and it was such a habit for him that I didn't even think about it. After he sniffed me tonight though, he pulled away and I could feel him staring at me while I tried my best to feign like I was asleep.

"Baby, why the fuck do you smell like gunpowder?" I didn't want to answer him so I started muttering like I was completely asleep and eventually, Trill just left it alone. I relaxed when I felt his head lay back down next to mine. I managed to get about four more hours of solid sleep before my phone started ringing. Usually, it would be turned off after a certain time, but I needed to make sure I was available for the hospital to update me at any time. Except this time, it wasn't the hospital. It was J3 and I knew something was wrong. Without even letting me say anything, he started to speak.

"Eryanna, you need to get down here right now. It's Drayven."

Running into the lobby with Trill jogging sluggishly behind, I wiped the sleep from my eyes as I approached the nurse's desk. I'd been there every day faithfully, so they knew me without me even having to check in and immediately took me back to the NICU where my nephew was being held. J3 saw Trill and I coming from down the hall and stood up to greet us. "I don't know what happened, Ery. He was fine, eating his bottle one moment, and seizing the next. They gave him medicine and they're running tests now." He explained. I had no choice but to have faith my nephew would be fine so I nodded my head and sat down while we waited for any news. If it wasn't one thing, it was another. Only about ten minutes after we arrived there, the doctor in charge of the floor at night came out, and I sighed at the grim look on his face.

"We've managed to stabilize him, but I do have to warn you... His heart stopped for over four minutes. That long without oxygen can cause severe brain damage." He explained as tears welled up in my eyes. My nephew was just an innocent baby. He didn't deserve any of this. The doctor wanted to say something else but every time he opened his mouth to say it, he shut it again and I was starting to become annoyed, just by looking at him. He looked like a fish out of water.

"What is it? Speak up." I snapped, as he seemed caught off guard by my bluntness.

"Well, I hate to ask this but it's necessary for our files. If the baby codes again, do you want us to resuscitate, even knowing that there's a seventy percent chance that he could be in a vegetative state for the rest of his life?" I guess I wasn't expecting him to say it like that so when those words came out of his mouth, I could've slapped the taste out of his mouth.

"Are you really asking me if you want me to save my nephew?" I questioned, looking around to see that everybody around me, even Trill, looked doubtful. "You guys aren't serious, right?" Staring dead in Trill's eyes, I stepped closer to him. I couldn't believe he wasn't taking my side.

"Baby, the doctor is saying that he won't do shit. He won't crawl, he won't be able to eat, talk or laugh. You really want that kind of life for a baby?"

"He said it's a possibility! But he doesn't know us. He doesn't know Drayven." I argued back. I didn't care what anybody in my family said, I would make sure the doctors saved my nephew. "You do everything you can for my nephew or you'll have the biggest lawsuit this hospital has ever seen." I warned him as I walked out, unable to believe the audacity of my family. It was still extremely early in the morning and it wasn't technically visiting hours, but I had to stop by and see how Jeryn was doing. A part of me hoped that I would walk in and see her talking shit, eating some weird ass thing and watching TV. Even though I knew that she wouldn't, it still hurt my heart to see her hooked up to those machines. Pulling up a chair beside her, I grabbed her hand and placed my head at her side like I'd done since we were little. "I don't know who you partying with or hanging with wherever you're at Jeryn, but I need you to come back now. We need you back now. I can't speak for everyone else but I'm going crazy without you. Being the strong one is your job. I can't do this." I began to sob, burying my face into the bed sheets. Right then, I felt my sister squeeze my hand but when I looked up, her eyes were still closed. Still, I knew that had to mean something so I went to the nurse's desk. "Can I get some help in my sister's room, please? I think she's waking up." Both of the nurses there grabbed their stethoscopes and ran to Jeryn's room. I joined them in the room but I hung in the background as they did their tests, tapping her feet and shining that light in her eyes. I saw the look that they'd given me, and more importantly, the look that they had given eachother. They thought I was crazy.

"Ms. January, I'm sorry to tell you this but there's been no change in your sister's condition. She's still unresponsive."

"That's not true. She squeezed my hand! She heard me talking to her! She squeezed my hand!"

"Muscle spasms in the hands and feet are common in cases like Jeryn's. I'm sorry, but visiting hours are over. You should leave now. I'll see you in a few hours." She apologized before walking out. I would have left like they said, but I had to give my sister a message first. I knew she was in there. Towering over Jeryn, I kissed her forehead and squeezed her hand one more time.

"I can feel you coming back to me, Jeryn. I don't care what they say and until you get better, I'll be right here."

# *Chapter Eleven:*

*"I been alone so long, I feel like I'm on the run."–Matt Maeson*

My nostrils flared and I couldn't even control the tears that ran down my face as my entire family sobbed. I couldn't get the image of him lying there like that out of my mind, and I knew that I never would. Azayo had put up a fight but by the time the ambulance arrived after my parents arrived and found him, he was already gone.

"Mama, everything is going to be alright." I choked as I walked over to my mother and embraced her. She stared at me blankly and I looked away since I knew I was lying. Things would never be okay again after this. She looked at me and for the first time, I saw all the hurt that I'd caused her written all over her face.

"How, Axl? How will anything ever be okay? Azayo is gone!" she screamed and I dropped my head. I knew it, and I was sure everyone else in my family knew it as well. This whole thing was my fault. Already knowing what time it was when I saw my brothers hustle into the other room, I followed behind them as they went to talk amongst themselves. There was chatter about who they thought did this, but we knew who it was. It was someone in the January family. Everyone's bet was on Jeryn, but I knew that was impossible, since I'd seen her with my own two eyes in the hospital.

"That bitch is a lot of things, but I don't think she's suicidal." Jaxn, my older brother, muttered as I shook my head. They didn't know that I'd been clocking Jeryn's every move but I wasn't about to say anything now. She couldn't have killed Azayo because she was in the hospital.

"Nah. Jeryn isn't going to just walk into our parents' house and shoot Azayo, who has nothing to do with any of this. That's not how she moves." Jeryn may have been one sneaky ass bitch, but I knew my brother was right. No matter how much of a disloyal bitch she was, Jeryn had her limits and she was the only person in the world who knew how much Zay really meant to me, and why he really meant so much to me. I headed to our security room since there was no point of pointing fingers when we had a top notch security system. Jaxn followed behind me, but the others stayed behind as we snuck off into the room. I wasn't a professional but I knew exactly what I was looking for and with Jaxn's help, we easily navigated through the frames until we found it. I watched the same frame over and over again, studying the figure in the black hoodie. It suddenly came to me, so I zoomed in when I noticed a distinct mark on the person's hand. I squinted, trying to make out what the tattoo was. I finally made out the outline of Trill's name, I got my gun ready. Since I had never liked Eryanna anyways so I would make sure that she paid for what she took from my family. Even if that meant I had to pick all of her family members off one by one. I had to play it smart because an all-out war could be a really stupid mistake on my part and I didn't want to do that. I decided to instead settle with sending a message so I called Jeremih. Just like his brother had been before he decided to sleep with my wife, Jeremih Hicks was a close friend of mine. When he picked up, I immediately started talking.

"What's good, my dawg?" I asked. When I heard him start to clear his throat, I began the next part of my speech. "I heard about your brother, man… We weren't exactly cool, but Jalen was a good guy. He didn't deserve that. Look, bro. I can't have you sitting up there all sad and shit. Me and the girls are having a barbecue. Bring the kids and stop by?" I baited, just wanting to hear what he had to say. I only had Jersei but if he said the word, I was pulling up. Not for a barbecue though.

"I wish I could but B got the kids. I'll catch you later though, man. I got shit to do." If he would have given me the time, I would have faked disappointment but Jeremih's lack of conversation gave me an opportunity to get my next task done. Since I'd picked up Jeremih plenty of times, I knew exactly where his baby mama stayed.

I couldn't figure out how Jeryn never knew about her long-lost sister. Though, I wasn't sure what was so long, or lost, about her. The moment that I saw Bellah, about a year after Jeryn and I got married, I knew she had some sort of relation to my wife. The similarities were too uncanny. She even acted just like a January. But it wasn't my business to say anything to Jeryn, so I didn't say anything. I secretly prayed that I would be around on the day, that Jeryn and Eryanna found out they weren't daddy's only little girls. It was unfortunate I missed it, but I would atone that now by watching the life slip away from their sister's lips. I pulled up and immediately walked up to their door to make sure I heard kids before I went back to my car and grabbed my automatic. I saw Bellah peek out of the window, that just meant she was closer to the window so that's where I needed to aim. Taking aim at the bedroom first, I wanted Bellah to watch her children die so I pulled the trigger and let off about fifteen bullets before moving my gun to the living room and letting off fifteen more shots until I was out of bullets. When I was certain that her house was quiet and everyone inside was dead, I drove away. Hopefully Eryanna got the message now. She was next.

# *Chapter Twelve:*

*"I've been waiting so long for a love like this." Summer Walker ft. Jhene Aiko*

The last thing I remembered was cradling my stomach so I wouldn't fall on it when I fell to the ground. I knew something wasn't right when I woke up. There were bright lights shining right in my eyes. The beeping of machines let me know I was in the hospital as I heard people passing by my room. That's when my hand instinctively went to my stomach and I noticed I was flat. There was no sign of life inside of me, and I freaked out.

"Oh, my God! My baby! My baby!" I shouted as I tried to pull every string I could find out of me. I relaxed when Eryanna ran up to my bedside and grabbed my hand.

"Relax, Jeryn. Everything is fine. Everything is okay." She said softly, rubbing my head as I leaned my head back into the pillow. Even if I had wanted to get up, I couldn't. The sharp throbbing in my pelvis was unbearable and immediately had me praying for it all to end.

"How can it be fine? Where is my baby?" I asked, trying not to shout since a nurse was just walking into my room.

"Oh, Ms. January, we've all been waiting for you to wake up. Welcome back." She smiled as I smiled weakly back at her, trying to be nice. I felt horrible and the only thing that would make me feel better was seeing my baby boy.

"Where is my baby?" I repeated again, closing my eyes as I waited for an answer that nobody was giving me. When I opened them again, Eryanna was scrolling through her phone as if she didn't hear me. She then showed me the screen of her phone and I immediately burst into tears. In the picture, Eryanna was holding the most beautiful baby boy I had ever seen. He had dark ringlets that framed his chubby face and even though he appeared so small in the pictures, I couldn't help but smile happily when I saw the rolls around his thighs.

"This was just yesterday. He's almost three pounds now. He's doing so good." She boasted proudly as my mouth dropped.

"Wait, how long have I been out?" I questioned, my mind racing with everything that I had probably missed in that time. All I could think about was how much my girls had missed me.

"Three weeks, one day and four hours. I've been

sitting here, singing to you and praying for God to make you feel better." Though she kept it very sweet, I could tell that I had missed a lot. I could see it in Eryanna's eyes. But then she continued to scroll and look at pictures of my baby and that made her smile. "By the way, I got tired of them calling him Baby January. I started calling him Drayven, but it's not on a birth certificate or anything..." She muttered with her head down. I could tell that she was unsure of my reaction, but words couldn't begin to explain how grateful I was for her holding shit down while I couldn't.

"He looks like a Drayven." I reassured my baby sister, grabbing her hand as we made eye contact. Looking around, I noticed the room was empty aside from us and frowned. Something didn't feel right. "Jalen hasn't been here?" I asked. Even on our worst terms, Jalen always came through for our daughter and I had no doubt that it would be the same for our son. The look on Eryanna's face told me something else was up. When she didn't say anything, I started to grow upset. "Ery, damn! Can you just tell me something? What's wrong? He locked up?" I begged. I could tell by the look on her face that she was worried about how I would respond to whatever she was about to say, but I didn't need her to worry. I needed her to tell me the truth that she was clearly hiding from me. I prepared myself for the worst when I watched Eryanna drop her head and take a deep breath.

"Jalen was shot. He's gone. I'm so sorry sis, but he's gone." She began to cry seeing the devastation written all over my face. My world came crashing down in that moment. Sure, Axl was my whole husband but Jalen was my world. I was in love with that man. It was so strange though, because no matter how much I sat there, it wasn't clicking. I must not have processed it entirely because tears would fall. Eryanna grabbed my hand but I snatched it away as my mind ran wildly with questions.

"Killed him? Are you sure it was him and not Jeremih? He wasn't strapped? Why didn't he have his piece?" I threw question after question Eryanna's way, because none of this was making any sense to me. She stayed quiet and I just knew things were about to get a whole lot worse.

"Jalen was coming from visiting you. He was in the hospital parking lot when someone gunned him down." Eryanna explained to me, barely able to get the words out. Throwing my head back, I willed the tears away that I just knew were coming. That's when I remembered how long my sister said that I had been out for.

"Eryanna, please don't tell me that I missed his funeral. Please don't tell me I missed my baby's funeral." I cried, refusing to believe that God would punish me like this. But Eryanna's face told me everything that I needed to know so I instantly began to sob.

"I'm sorry, Jeryn… It was yesterday." All of the will that I had to keep it together vanished in that moment and before I knew it, I was fighting three nurses, a security guard and Eryanna, just to get out of my bed. I had to get out of the hospital. I had to get somewhere. There was nothing I could do from inside those walls and I needed to find out who took Jalen away from me, his kids and the plethora of people who loved him. I had a feeling that I had an idea who was responsible, but Jalen was a dope-boy. He had a few associates, a couple of friends and a lot of enemies. Anybody could have killed him. Just as I was about to ask her what the streets were saying, a nurse walked in and my mind shifted to something brighter.

"Excuse me, but can I be taken to my baby? I want to see my son and I've been asking everybody." I asked politely. Something told me that the nurses already knew our circumstances because she gave me a sad nod and went to grab a wheelchair. I didn't even notice anything was different until I tried to get up and realized I was handcuffed to the bed. That's when all the past events came rushing back and I began to cry, remembering everything that happened at the police station and what they were accusing me of. It was just my sister and I in the room, now so it was my chance to be vulnerable. I never allowed anyone else to see that side of me. "I didn't kill that girl, Eryanna. I swear I didn't. I wanted to, you know that. But I didn't touch her." I confessed and Eryanna just nodded, rubbing my head to try and calm me down like my mother did when we were younger.

"Don't worry, I know. I know you, Jeryn. I know you're not capable of that and we'll get through this. We'll make it past this. I promise." Three weeks I was out must have really matured Eryanna because she was usually the one coming to me when she needed calming, not the other way around. However, she just seemed so serene like nothing was bothering her. I knew exactly why when she stood up. I could tell that I had been out awhile because I was seeing Eryanna's stomach for the first time and it was huge.

"Goddamn." Was all I could blurt out as I eye-balled her basketball-shaped belly. Eryanna began to laugh as she reached beside my bed and grabbed a bag. Putting it into my lap, she watched in anticipation as I opened it. I was close to tears when I pulled out a blue teddy bear.

"Let's just say that there's no doubt I'm carrying Trill's son. The lil nigga was playing with his dick in the ultrasound." My eyes nearly bulged out of my head when the nurse walked in but it didn't seem like she was paying us any mind, so I couldn't help but laugh out loud.

"Sounds more like his mom than his dad to me." I howled, unable to control my laughter. Eryanna shot me her middle finger and that only succeeded in making the joke funnier. When I was finally wheeled into the nursery, it shocked the fuck out of me to see Trill standing there, watching my son intently with all those blue scrubs on. The nurse saw my surprised expression and chuckled herself.

"Uncle Trei here has not left little man's side. You might be in for a rude awakening because he's the only one who can get this little fellow to act right." She joked as Eryanna and I both laughed. I could tell that it relaxed my sister to see how good her boo was with my baby. That meant he'd be a thousand times greater when it was time for their baby to be born. When Trill turned my way, I was expecting him to say something stupid and you know Trill. He never disappoints.

"They had to tie your son's IV to his arm, 'cause he kept trying to take it out. Lil dude bad as fuck already." He said loudly, causing my son to cry. I almost rushed to him but then Eryanna grabbed my arm as I watched Trill. "My bad, my bad. I was just joking. Lil dawg, relax. You good with me." He cooed, rubbing Drayven's hand as he calmed down immediately. I almost started bawling at how sweet that moment was, until a detective walked in and ruined the moment.

"Ms. January?" Walking right up on me, I prepared for them to put my hands behind my back and whisk me away, but he didn't do that. Instead, he regretfully handed me a paper and a wide grin spread over my face as I read what they were telling me. I could see the anger was written all over the officer's face and it pained him to give me good news, but I was rejoicing on the inside. Trill noticed everything going on and walked over to us while Eryanna, who was still behind me, reading over my shoulder. I kept my celebration on the inside but Eryanna, who was the loud, ratchet, opposite version of me, spoke out loud.

"What is it? What's going on?" Trill asked, as I finished up the letter. Before I could say anything, Eryanna beat me to it.

"The district attorney decided not to file charges on Jeryn. They said there was too many conflicting pieces of evidence, but none directly pointing to her." I had always hated when Eryanna did that but when she cut me off this time, I couldn't do anything but laugh. Even just by laughing too hard, it caused the pain in my pelvis to intensify. I had my daughters naturally so this C-section pain was new for me. The nurse saw my discomfort and forced me to get back in my wheelchair. Since I couldn't hold him yet, I decided to go back to my room. Once Eryanna and Trill got me back in the bed and as comfortable as I was going to get, I could tell there was something else that she wanted to tell me. This was Eryanna, so I knew I wouldn't have to wait long. The medicine they gave me was strong as hell because I could feel it kicking in almost as soon as I got in the bed. Trill left and that's when Eryanna grabbed my hand.

"I did something really bad, Jeryn." She confessed. "Before you say something, I just want to say… I really wanted to get back at Axl. He put us through so much and I… I needed to do something to make him pay." The more that Eryanna talked, the more I could tell that she had really fucked up. I could feel my mouth getting dry so I reached for my ice cup and just as I felt the coolness of ice touching my tongue, she started talking again. "I killed Azayo, Jeryn. I shot him in his head." She murmured, only loud enough so that I could hear her. I hadn't expected her to say that so the answer caused me to choke on the ice as it cascaded down my throat. When I finally caught my breath again, I repeated what she had said back to me.

"You killed Azayo, who? Eryanna, please do not tell me we are not talking about Azayo Bailey." I growled, gritting my teeth. The look in her eyes told me everything I needed to know. My sister had no idea what she had started.

I was about to reveal a deep dark secret that only I

knew, but it was important. She needed to know how serious this was. "He thought he was going to get away with this, so I took his brother from him. I had to show him not to play with us. If he keeps it up, I'll show his brothers too."

"No, you didn't! Eryanna, you have no idea what you've done. You started a war. You didn't kill Axl's baby brother. You killed Axl's son."

*"So don't judge me like your honor," –Meek Mill*

After making sure that Jeryn was settled in and that she had been given enough medicine to put her back to sleep for the night, I headed home to take a shower and get some decent food in my stomach. After being folded up on a chair for almost a month straight, my son and I needed to sleep in an actual bed. With J3 at the hospital for the night, keeping an eye on Jeryn, Jeidyn and Draven in case anything went wrong, and Bellah meeting him there later, I knew that they would be able to handle everything for only a night while I relaxed. I managed to make it into my house and get to the kitchen to eat some almost-spoiled pineapple before my phone started going off. I didn't recognize the number but I knew it was someone local by the area code so I answered it. Hearing Bellah on the other line, I rolled my eyes until I heard the fear in her voice. That immediately concerned me so I swept my annoyance to the side briefly.

"Eryanna, I'm so- I'm sorry. I know you don't really like me, but I didn't know who else to call. J3 wasn't answering." One of my many gifts was being able to read a person and I could tell that Bellah was scared out of her mind. Her voice was shaky and she was trying hard not to choke on her words. "He shot- he shot up my house. My kids!" She began to cry, rambling about some other stuff that I couldn't understand. I immediately grabbed my keys. She was surrounded by silence and since I knew from my own experiences that kids were hardly ever quiet, I could only think the worst.

"Who's he? Who shot up your house, Bellah?" I asked, while I tried to calm her down enough to understand what she was actually saying. She only got more hysterical when I asked that question, so I took a deep breath. "Where are you, Bellah?" I asked as I got into my car and turned on my GPS. I could drive for forever, but without a destination, it wouldn't make a difference. That's when it really hit me that Bellah was supposed to be my sister and I didn't even know a simple thing about her, like where she lived. I knew nothing about her. When her text alert finally came to my phone and I saw the address, I turned my car around and went the opposite way. All I could think about while I drove was that if something had happened to Bellah's kids, their blood was on my hands because I had basically treated their mother like a stranger and not my blood sister. I was afraid of change and had pushed them away. Bellah didn't have to say who 'he' was. In my heart, I knew it was Axl getting back at me because I had killed Azayo. I knew that the only way to end this was to end Axl once and all so I rampaged through our home, looking for Trill's secret stash of guns. I knew he had some hidden somewhere. I searched every crevice of every room and still couldn't find anything, so I did the next best thing. I called Trill and asked him. I was so out of breath from looking that by the time Trill answered the phone, I felt like an elephant was sitting on my chest. "Where are your guns, Trill? I know they're somewhere around here." I yelled, still searching while Trill laughed about it with his friends. I could tell that I was on speaker and being the center of their joke infuriated me. I instantly stood up. "Look, I don't know what you and your boys are doing but I'm serious Trei," I scolded him, calling him by his real name so he knew I was serious. "Someone just shot up Bellah's house, while her and her kids were in there and I'ma just say this... You can come with me or you can stay out of it but either way, I'm going to finish this. I'm tired of his shit." I explained to Trill. He seemed to finally take me serious then.

"Wait, what? Ery, no. Mama, hold on. Just wait until I get there." He begged, but I wasn't hearing any of that. I wasn't a weak bitch when Trill met me, and I for sure wasn't about to turn into one now. I didn't need a nigga's protection to still get the job done.

"Fuck that! Wait for what, Trill? Wait for him to

shoot someone else I love? Kill someone else I love? I'm tired of this nigga and he needs to be handled! What if he kills you, Trill? What if he tries to shoot me? What will I do?"

"Eryanna, please don't do anything until I get there." Trill begged and I could hear noises behind him that I assumed were from him driving. "I'm four minutes away, ma. Don't do anything until I get there." Trill could do all the talking he wanted but at this point, I wasn't listening. All I could think about was all of the hurt that Axl had caused us. There was only way, that I knew, to get rid of him and start to heal my family.

# Chapter Fourteen:

*"Every morning, we trappin' and then we kill at night." -*
*Calboy*

Today was definitely a cause for celebration. After a month and a week of being admitted in the hospital, Jeidyn and I were finally going home. It had been hell sitting beside her every day, knowing that she was hurt and it was my fault. That was okay though because I promised myself when I got my hands on Axl, he was going to pay for what he did to my baby girl. Since I knew Jeidyn was coming home with me today, my anxiety was partially relieved. I still didn't feel right going home without Baby Drayven though. Eryanna had secured us a new townhome while I was unable to do it and moved everything in by herself. I was confident that everything else was under control as well. I could tell that her and J3 were doing their thing and I appreciated that, because I knew things would be tight for me until I could start making runs again. I didn't know when that would be. I was feeling a lot better than before still unlike myself. Drayven made it all worth it though. Eryanna wasn't lying. He was the most beautiful baby I had ever laid my eyes on.

All of the nurses in the hospital had grown to love Jeidyn because of her loud and sassy personality so when I brought her into the NICU so that I could hold Dray before I left, they were all thrilled.

"Alright mommy's girl," I began, wincing as I squatted down so that I was as close to eye level as I could be with my three-year old. "Remember what mommy said about baby brother right?" I questioned, making sure that she understood she couldn't go into his room being loud. He was doing well and everyone was confident that he would be able to come home in a week or so. But they still had some concerns. The first hearing test that they administered, Drayven had no reaction too, so his doctor decided to run one more test. I wasn't sure when so until they did, I would just have to wait patiently for my baby boy to come home.

Jeidyn nodded and I gave her a kiss on her cheek, wobbling and struggling to get back on my feet. I wasn't recovering as quickly as I had hoped and for someone like me who's used to always being on the go, it was hard for me to learn to sit my ass down somewhere. Even with Dom constantly reminding me to take it easy. For the past month that I had been sitting in this hospital bed, awake and bored, he had been here, just making sure I was good. I had never met him before this but I knew that he was a good friend of

Bellah's. Dom was genuinely a sweet guy and he made me laugh so hard that I would end up snorting. I could tell that he wanted something more out of me but I wasn't capable of giving it to him. I couldn't even be all there for my kids at this moment. My two youngest no longer had a father and if I had my way, Jersei's dad would soon be gone too. My babies only had me left so I had no choice but to go hard. After washing me and Jeidyn's hands, I sat down and opened my shirt as the nurse brought me my son to cuddle. "How's my handsome man doing today?" I cooed as I ran my fingers through his hair, even though I was talking to the nurse. When she placed him on my chest, I began to feel complete like only a mother could. By the smile on the nurse's face, I could tell she was about to give me some good news.

"The doctor did Drayven's second hearing test today and everything seemed fine. They think that the machine was faulty because a couple of the other babies got weird results as well." She explained and that news made me smile because I knew it was only a matter of time now before Drayven would be coming home to be with me and his sisters. "Also, he's drinking almost two ounces at a time all by himself, so we're getting there. Just hold on, mama." She encouraged me as she watched me stroke my son's hair, humming some random lullabye as I watched my son relax up against my chest and drift off to sleep. It didn't matter how impatient I was becoming about getting my baby home with me, I knew the most important thing was him being healthy. Right then, I heard a knock on the door and I didn't even have to look up to know who it was.

"Come in, Ery." Both the nurse and I laughed because we had an inside joke around here that Eryanna was trying to kidnap my baby. She was with him more than I was, but I never said anything. In all honesty, I was thankful that she loved him the way that she did when I wasn't able to do it. I could tell they had a special bond by the way he opened his eyes and looked around whenever he heard her voice. As she walked in, dark bags were under her eyes. I knew my sister better than she knew herself and I could tell by the look on her face that whatever was going on, wasn't for nosey ears to hear. When the nurse excused herself to continue her rounds, Eryanna plopped herself down next to me. "What's wrong?" I asked, assuming her and Trill had been at it again. With the baby coming sooner rather than later, the two had been beefing. I could only imagine that Eryanna spending all her time here was starting to put a strain on their relationship.

"It's Kisa. She's missing," Eryanna began to explain before I cut her off, thinking I could solve the problem easily.

"Did you and J3 check the location? All their phones have-," I ordered before she waved me off, shutting me up instantly.

"We already did." She responded and by the loud, tired sigh that escaped her mouth, I knew that it was only about to get worse. "Axl has her." My jaw dropped and I frantically rushed to press the nurse's button. When she ran in, I could tell that she was confused because I never called them while I was loving on Drayven. I quickly passed my son back over to her arms.

"I need to get home. Can you take him please?" Once he was cuddled back in his incubator, I leaned in to talk to him while I buttoned my shirt back up. "Mommy is coming back, Dray. I promise you. I just gotta handle some stuff first, but I'll be back before you close your eyes for the night. I promise." I whispered to him before shutting the door of the incubator and leading my younger sister out of the room. Jeidyn followed behind us, her hand attached to mine, as we talked amongst ourselves.

"I'm going to handle Axl, once and for all. I'ma get Kisa and end all of this. I'm tired of him and if I give him the opportunity, he's going to make my life hell." I whispered as we made it to the car where Trill was waiting in the front seat. I did my best not to alert my young daughter as to what was going on. She had already been through enough. I quickly strapped Jeidyn in to her carseat and just as I was about to get in the passenger's side so he could drive off, a car honking caught my attention. I looked up just in time to see J3's car speeding up to his. He barely stopped in time to keep from hitting me, quickly put the car in park and then hopped out, walking up to Eryanna's window. I looked at J3 and frowned when he mouthed the words, "It's Axl" to me. I snatched the phone and became disgusted when I heard Axl snickering like the bitch he was.

"Now why would you do that? You always were a nosey bitch. Hand the phone back to Eryanna." He ordered and I shook my head like he could see me. I was sure that by now, he knew Ery had killed Azayo, but I had no intention of letting my sister meet up with him, just so he could kill her. I knew how Axl got down. Since I knew how he operated, I did my best to plead with him to see our side of things.

"You already killed my dad and Jalen, Axl! You tried to kill my daughter! My baby! Why are you doing this? It's an eye for an eye, a life for a life! We're even. It's done. It's over." I tried to persuade him. Axl laughing caused my stomach to flip. It disturbed my soul to the point that I caught chills.

"You don't even know the kind of damage that your sister caused when she killed Zay. We'll never be even and I put my life on that. Not until I rob you of everyone you love and you get to watch them die a slow agonizing death... and trust me, as much as I would love to take credit for watching Jalen's life seep out onto the concrete outside the hospital you were laying in, that wasn't me." After he was finished talking, I heard the sounds of Kisa screaming and pleading in the background. "It's either this bitch or your sister. You said your girls are like family, right? Well, prove it. It's time to choose." Then, I was met with the sound of the dial-tone. Eryanna turned around, clearly trying to figure out how the conversation went, but I had nothing to say as my mind went into overdrive. Now we were back to square one and Axl clearly had the advantage.

# Chapter Fifteen:

*"Treat you like I never knew you. Put it on your head." –*
*Meek Mill*

As soon as I got off of the phone with Jeryn, I chucked my phone across the room. Kisa immediately stopped crying, crawled over and put her head in my lap as I patted her like she was a dog. In a sense, she was. That was my bitch.

"I gotta watch you, Kisa. I see you good at acting." I laughed, as she struggled to pull my belt out from its loops. Kisa had been on my team since she was fifteen, which nobody else knew because that's the way I liked it. Jeryn recruiting her meant that it gave me an advantage. For three years almost, I had learned everything about how the January Cartel ran their trap. Kisa was quiet enough to remain in the background undetected but dominant enough to take control when she needed to. I loved that shit.

Throwing my belt to the ground, she took me in her mouth and I grabbed all of the hair that I could fit and pulled it as hard as I could. Kisa could fight me all she wanted to, but I knew the truth. She liked that shit. She was gagging and choking, but that only meant her mouth was getting wetter. I took it out and slapped her a few times with it, proceeding to fuck her throat again when she collected enough spit. Just as I was about to cum, I pulled her off of me and she assumed the position, standing up and bending over to grab her ankles. That's one thing I loved about her young ass. She was flexible as fuck. But I got distracted when I looked up at my TV and saw the news that a young toddler had been found, near death. When they showed the location and it was exactly where I left Jeidyn, I instantly went soft and cursed under my breath. I thought I had killed that little pest, so her being alive was just another loose end I had to tie up. With it being plastered all over the news, I knew that it was only a matter of time before they found out something. It was time to do some damage control.

I pulled out of Kisa and immediately wrote down the hotline number, quickly calling them, knowing it was time to start putting out the fire that I knew was coming my way. Kisa stood by anxiously, waiting to see what I was going to do as she threw on her robe.

"Hey, about that little girl you just found… A homeboy of mine started talking about a little girl he kidnapped. I don't know his real name, but we call him Carlo on the streets. No, I'd like to remain anonymous. Thank you." Quickly hunging up, I made sure that I kept my conversation short so that they wouldn't have enough time to track my location. Looking at the clock, I cussed again when I realized I was late. I was supposed to be meeting my parents at the funeral home for Azayo in a little less than twenty minutes to pay for the service. Throwing Kisa's clothes at her, I ignored her sulking at our time being cut short again. "I promise baby, after I get the blood off my hands, it won't be like this no more. It will be just me and you, for sure." She rolled her eyes and folded her arms, pouting like a baby. I had to remind myself that she was barely legal and still learning. Otherwise, I would've smacked the shit out of her.

"Yeah. I've heard that before. That's what you said before Harmony! Remember that? Why am I your main option now?" she questioned me. Instead of answering her, I spun her around and looked her in the eyes. I could see her hard core melting as she became a little less irritated with me.

"I love you, Ki."

"I love you too, daddy." When I was sure everything was okay between us, I left and went to meet my parents so that we could make the final arrangements for Azayo's service. I had picked out a fresh ass suit for my son and so far, I had done a good job of keeping it together for the rest of the family. But before meeting my parents, I knew I needed to check in with my brothers and do something Kisa would definitely not approve of. My parents were still working on preparing the service for my son, so my brothers and I were focused on making sure some other families would need services too, starting with Eryanna and Jeryn. With a huge smile on my face, I sped off to meet with Jaxn and the others so we could discuss how we were going to do this. All I knew was that it was time for them to pay.

# Chapter Sixteen:

*"You won't commit a crime bigger than giving me up." -
NIKI*

Jeryn knew exactly where Axl would be and she
thought she could outsmart me and try to sneak off without
me, but there was no way I was going to allow her to handle
Axl by herself. Trill was on edge and had hired bodyguards
to follow us everywhere, but dodging them was nothing I
wasn't already used to. Jeryn and I spent most of our teenage
years doing that. I knew that if Trill got word of me riding
along with Jeryn, he would definitely flip out so I turned my
phone off. If it came down to it, I'd tell him I was at Lamaze
class, since that was the one place he refused to go anyways.
At the end of the day, Jeryn was my sister and there was no
way that I was letting her go solo. Just as she was about to
pull off, I got into her passenger's seat and she seemed
surprised, but she didn't argue against me coming.
Surprisingly, she actually seemed relieved that she wouldn't
be by herself.

"You better make sure Trill never finds out about this

or he'll kill both of us for endangering his kid." She laughed but I could tell she was only half-joking. With good reason too. Trill was crazy goofy and he played about a lot of things, but his kids weren't one of them. I knew him well and if something happened to this baby because of me, he would definitely beat my ass for being careless. Right as we pulled off into traffic, Dom called me and Eryanna side-eyed me while smirking, like she knew something I didn't. I already knew what she was thinking, so I flicked her off and answered the phone. "Hey, you." I flirted, smacking my lips when Ery began to cackle loudly like a hyena. She was cock-blocking and didn't even know it. "Sorry Dom, that's my dumb-ass sister. How are you? How's your day going?" she questioned and I could only laugh when I heard some questionable noise in Dom's background as well. It was good to know Jeryn wasn't the only one who had a lot going on at the moment. I had been messing with my sister a lot about her new crush but the smile on her face told me that she liked Dom, at least enough to be his friend and that was good enough for me. I honestly felt it was best if she took it slow before jumping into something else.

Dom was just about to respond and that's when Jeryn got a call on another line. I was surprised to hear Kisa's voice flow through the Bluetooth speaker and engulf her car. She seemed out of breath and her voice was shaking like she had been running from something. "Kisa, are you alright? Where are you?" she rambled, shooting question after question her way. We didn't hear anything for a minute, so Jeryn took her phone off the Bluetooth and began calling Kisa's name. The connection was shaky and all I heard was static until her voice came through softly. Jeryn then reconnected her Bluetooth so I could hear what was going on as well.

"Jeryn, are you there?" she whispered. Her voice was shaking and I didn't even want to imagine what Axl was doing to her, all because of me. Guilt settled in my stomach and I rubbed on my small baby bump, just trying to calm my baby down. Whenever I got stressed, he'd put himself in a little ball and that shit hurt like a bitch. Before Jeryn could say anything, Kisa began explaining everything and my jaw dropped at what she revealed. "Jeryn, I- I can't talk for long. I can't let him know what is going on. But I just want to tell you I'm sorry." She said more than that, but that was the only part I understood because after that, she began sobbing like a baby. She rambled for a moment before giving us the address of where to meet her and then she hung up.

I had no idea what she was apologizing for, but seeing the look on Jeryn's face, she knew exactly what was going on. Her jaw was clenched and watching her fists grip the steering wheel let me know that she was pissed. She made a quick U-turn and all I could do was hold on so that I wouldn't fly out of the window. As soon as she got to where we needed to be, she hopped out and barely turned the car off. I followed behind her. I never noticed Jeryn grab her piece, but I noticed it in her waistband as we walked up the sidewalk and looked around. That's when I saw Kisa and she ran to us. Instead of embracing her like a little sister, my sister kept Kisa at arms' length, staring her down like she was our enemy. Her facial expression never changed and she remained cold and emotionless while she waited for Kisa to find her words. "Jeryn, I…. I-," Stuttering, I could already tell that Kisa knew she was in the wrong by how nervous she was. Then, right in broad daylight, my sister took out her gun and shot Kisa right in the chest, so close that as she stumbled for a second before falling face-down to the ground, I saw smoke leave her body. That's when we both ran back to the car, as fast as my swollen legs would take me. I had no idea what was going on but by the time I turned to Jeryn, she was already waving me off like she knew what I was going to say.

"Kisa was working with him. I've been known… this just confirmed it. Sometimes you have to kill the messenger too." She explained, quoting our dad which immediately shut me up. We drove off and parked as Jeryn got on the phone to find someone who would handle the cleanup. It was weird watching her smile and act like she hadn't just killed someone moments before, and for just a second, I questioned if my sister was losing her mind. Dom called and the smile on my sister's face distracted me from anything else I was about to say. She answered on the second ring like an anxious schoolgirl. I hadn't seen that smile on her face since I watched her fall in love with Jalen. Unfortunately, that smile went away fast when I tapped her on her shoulder after seeing some people walk up to our car out of the corner of my eye. The entire mood changed, but Jeryn remained calm as she looked around and quickly locked the car doors. That didn't make a difference. There were four of them outside of the car and two of us inside, and I could tell just by their stature that all four of them were men. Jeryn and I had no chance. We'd have no choice but to shoot them. I followed Jeryn's lead and stayed stone-faced as she quickly tried to reverse the car and get us both out of there. That was no use. As soon as she backed out, something hard hit the back window and shattered it. One of them was holding a bat and intent on not letting us go anywhere. We both screamed and that's when Dom got involved.

"Where are you, Jeryn? Where are you?" he asked as I heard the urgency in his voice and that let me know that he was about to come for us, which relieved me. We only had to hold on until he got to us. Jeryn quickly shouted out the address where we were, as we both grabbed guns from underneath the seat as the same time. Right when we were about to start spraying, I felt someone choking me from behind with my seatbelt strap and I struggled to get my fingernails underneath just enough to get some air flowing. I swung my arms behind my seat to try and fight whoever was holding my seatbelt, but it was no use. They were a lot taller than me and they had the advantage since they were right behind me. I couldn't tell what Jeryn was doing because I couldn't turn my head, but I heard her yelling and fighting so I was sure that they had gotten her too. I was still fighting to breathe even though my vision started to blur and just as I thought I was going to pass out, I managed to feel around and unclasp my seatbelt, swinging my arm around behind me. Whoever it was behind me, I hit them hard enough to catch him off guard, but his shock didn't last long enough for me to gain the advantage. He quickly grabbed the gun that had fallen beside me and pointed it right at me. All I could think about was if God would forgive me for putting my innocent baby boy in harm's way and never giving him a chance to live his life. Then I watched the man slowly pull the trigger.

# Chapter Seventeen:

*"God made a Goddess. Grab my arm and know that I got you." -Wale*

I had been ambushed enough times to know what was going on and more importantly, I recognized the voices of the men behind the masks. They could try and play games if they wanted to, but I had spent enough time with Axl's brothers to know each and every one of their voices. Jaxn was the one who had his arm around my throat and I fought to keep my air flowing as I reached beside me to look for my piece that had somehow gotten lost in the fight. As I grabbed it and tried to aim, still fighting to get Jaxn off of me, I heard tires screeching to a drastic and sudden stop behind my car. I would've tried to look up, but it wouldn't have made a difference. With Jaxn's strong arms around my throat, my vision was starting to get blurry. I looked up into my rearview mirror just in time to see the outline of Dom and his boys coming to our rescue.

*"Thank God,"* I praised silently, just as a crazy shoot-out erupted between both Dom's group and Axl's brothers.

All Eryanna and I could do was try and lay low while more than twenty shots rang out. Our windows started to shatter, and I could feel bullets hitting our car so I I threw my car in reverse, getting out and down the street, just in time to see the police speeding towards the parking lot. I became nervous thinking about Dom and if he got out of there in time, but relaxed when I saw his car trailing a safe distance behind me. He even stuck his hand out of the window to wave at me and to make sure I knew he was alright. "We made it, Ery! We made it!" I screamed, cheering and laughing like a robber who had just pulled off the ultimate heist. Until I looked over at Eryanna, who dead quiet and not saying anything. Her eyes widened in horror and I followed her gaze to her stomach. I didn't see anything at first until I watched my sister's hand, which was pressed over her belly, and blood stained her caramel-colored hands. "No, no, no, no… Don't worry, I got you." I quickly put my seatbelt back on and sped off. I would've stayed back and called 911, but I knew I could get her to the hospital quicker. We didn't have time to wait around for an ambulance. I was right too. In the time that it would've taken for the ambulance just to get to us, I was swerving into the emergency room parking lot so quickly that smoke should've been under my tires. I had called Dom to let him know about the situation. Now, he was on his way to meet us at the hospital. By this time, the shock had vanished and Eryanna's hands were shaking as she kept pressure on her wound.

"My baby…" she cried, as I did my best to reassure her that everything would be okay. All her color had left her body and I could tell that she was getting weaker by the moment. I put my car in park as fast as I could and ran into the emergency room, immediately grabbing the nurses' attention by the amount of blood on my hands.

"Someone help me, please! My sister's been shot and she's pregnant. She's outside, please help me!" I begged loudly. Three nurses ran behind me, one with a gurney, as I showed them where my car was. They pulled Eryanna out as she cried out in pain and though I reassured her everything was going to be okay, I couldn't help but curse myself out for letting her even come with me. All of this was my fault and right about now, I wasn't even sure that everything would work out. I knew that holding onto my faith was important, but when it came to my sister and my kids, I could only pray for the best but expect the worst. I was starting to get used to bad things happening, but I would never be able to forgive myself for this.

Now, I understood how Eryanna felt while she waited for the doctor to update her on me because I was going crazy as I stared at the clock. I called J3 and Bellah, who both confirmed that they were on their way. It seemed like hours but only minutes had passed and then I saw Dom enter the hospital. Before he could even enter the waiting room all the way, I was running into his arms. Ever since my father had passed away, I prided myself on being strong and not wearing my heart on my sleeve. I never needed any help from a man, not even the man I was married to. With Dom, it was different. I felt protected, like it was possible to be the soft, vulnerable woman I was meant to be and finally let a man take control. We were just friends and friends only, but I knew that if I let him take it there and given him the green light, he would claim me as his with no hesitation. It was written all over his face and in his eyes. Maybe one day, I would give him a chance but after everything with Jalen, I couldn't see myself being with anyone for awhile. A very long while.

Being with Dom made the waiting game easier. Rather than driving myself crazy, I passed the time by showing Dom pictures of Eryanna and I when we were kids, and showed him how much my kids favored her. My oldest daughter acted just like Eryanna, and Jeidyn looked just like her. To the point that when we went out, people always assumed my youngest daughter was hers. Dom kept me laughing and time passed by quickly. Before I knew it, the doctor was coming up to us and I could tell that bad news was coming too. We had been in that hospital so much that I guess everyone already knew who we were. The doctor didn't even ask to confirm if Eryanna was my sister before she started to explain the situation to Dom and I.

"Luckily for everyone involved, Ms. January is okay. The bullet missed all of her major arteries and organs, but we did run into a significant problem along the way. One of the two bullets tore into one of your sister's babies. We were able to remove the bullet, but we couldn't save the baby. I'm sorry." I felt nauseous and weak as I thought about the devastating loss I had caused my sister and dropped to my knees, as Dom did his best to catch me, letting me process the information. The doctor stood there and then something that she had said, finally registered to me.

"What do you mean 'one of the babies'? My sister was only having one baby." I frowned, sure that they had made a mistake. Leading me away so that we were talking privately and out of the way of everyone else, I waited for someone to tell me that I was being punked when we got to the hallway.

"Ms. January, I believe that what happened here is known as superfetation," she began to explain, chuckling at the confusion written all over my face. "It's when two separate eggs are fertilized weeks apart from the same ovulation cycle… So basically, what we have here, and what your sister is experiencing, is twins with two different due dates. She had two babies with two different gestational ages. I suspect that the reason none of the doctors caught this, was because your sister's twins are a significant amount of time apart. I'm talking about four to five weeks apart, which is extremely uncommon. The older boy took the bullet and was unable to be saved. Well, let's just say if everything goes well from here, which I suspect it will, Twin B should arrive around his due date, healthy." I had never heard of anything like what the doctor was talking about, so I just nodded like I knew what was going on. "You can see your sister now, but be brief. We had to give her a sedative so she could relax and stop crying." She smiled, patted my back and then walked away as I went to find Eryanna. It only took a few seconds to find where she was and as I stared in the doorway and watched my baby sister fight back tears while she stared at a piece of paper in her hand, my heart broke for her, and for the pain that I had caused. Even with the surprise of Eryanna carrying twins, it didn't take away the hurt of knowing only one of her twins would be born alive and healthy. She seemed to notice my presence and momentarily looked up, but immediately dropped her head back down. I went right to her side.

"Eryanna, I am so fucking sorry…" I started to cry. I

could only wonder if my sister wouldn't look at me, because in her heart, she blamed me too. She remained strong and solid for a second, but watching her sit there was like watching the planes crash on September 11th. You knew complete and utter destruction was inevitable and coming your way fast. She covered her face with her hands and broke down, while I stared at her helplessly. There was nothing I could do to ease her pain, even though I wanted to.

"The nurse is about to call Trill." She sobbed and I laid my head on her, knowing exactlywhat that meant. He was going to come to the hospital, find out what went down, and then it was going to be over for Eryanna and Trill.

The sedatives quickly knocked Eryanna out but I stayed beside her anyways. I knew she would need some type of support with Trill coming, and luckily for her, I heard him coming from all the way down the hallway. I was in the hallway when he walked up to me, because I knew how Trill could get and no matter how he felt about the situation, Eryanna still needed to rest. He could say whatever he needed to say later. She had a long road to recovery to go, both physically and emotionally. Trill saw me and stormed towards me, but even the fire in his eyes wouldn't make me move from the door.

"What the fuck happened? Someone just started

busting out of nowhere??" he questioned. I didn't want to lie but I also knew that the hospital, around countless police officers, nurses, and doctors, wasn't the place to converse about this particular topic. He could tell by my hesitation that something wasn't right and backed me up into the corner. I had never been scared of Trill before and I wasn't scared now, but the rage in his eyes was something different for me. I finally realized the 'other side' that my sister was referring to. When he pushed past me, I let him. Usually, I wouldn't have moved but Eryanna still needed to have a conversation with him to tell him about the baby, and I knew it wouldn't go well so I stayed outside in case she needed reinforcements. I wasn't listening in on their conversation but just by glancing through the window, I could read their lips. I saw Eryanna break the news of their baby, while trying to tell him the good news about their unexpected arrival. I also watched as he punched a wall and got so far in Eryanna's face that I thought he was going to lay his hands on her. Just as I walked in to intervene and make sure things didn't get out of hand, Trill flew towards me so fast that I flinched. He gritted his teeth and backed me up into the wall in the corner of the room. The blinds were closed so nobody on the outside could see what was going on. His teeth were clenched together and I prepared for him to threaten to kill me, but he must have thought better of it and just stormed away. Peering back into the room, the devastation written all over my sister's face was undeniable and I rushed to her side. I had no idea what I could do to help her at this moment, but I would try whatever was necessary. I held her head to my chest as she sobbed and I struggled with words that would help her feel better.

"I'm going to fix this. I promise." I continued to comfort my sister while I dazed off. The only thing that made me feel better was the thought of torturing Axl for the pain he had caused Ery.

# Chapter Eighteen:

*"You know me well from the nightmares of an empty cell."*
*–Jay-Z*

A mango. They said that my son, Ezrah Tristyn Monroe, wasn't any bigger than a large mango. As much as I tried to ignore the tragedy and focus on the fact that I still had a baby to care for and love on, I couldn't help but stare at the ultrasound picture that the nurses had given me when they realized he wouldn't make it. At nineteen weeks, my son wasn't considered viable. That meant they didn't perform any life-saving surgeries because the likelihood of him surviving them was slim. The good news was that because my sons were created at two different times, they had separate amniotic sacs and so the doctors were able to remove Ezrah so that his body wouldn't decompose and make his brother or me sick. He was a chunky little guy, weighing almost fourteen ounces and he was tall like Trill too, eleven inches long. The nurses cleaned him up to the best of their ability, and then brought him later so that Trill and I could take turns holding him. Once J3 and Bellah heard about what was going on, they joined Jeryn at the hospital to say their goodbyes. A pastor even came in to pray and then they took Ezrah away. Four days later, here I was being wheeled out of the hospital to go home and I couldn't focus on giving God praise on anything. Yes, he had spared my life and the life of one of my sons, but that didn't take away the hurt of him taking one of my babies from me. Jeryn helped me into the car and took me home since she had already been there visiting Drayven, and nobody could get in contact with Trill. I hadn't talked to him since he left the hospital. I knew he was angry with me. I was angry with me, too. With that being said, the only way we were going to get through this was to stick together, but I hadn't seen Trei since I had to give him the surprising news that though we were having twins, we had lost one. I would never forget the amount of hurt that appeared in his eyes and if looks could kill, I would've been dead. As a matter of fact, I was pretty sure that if we had that conversation anywhere else, my sister would have definitely been burying me. Luckily for me though, Trill was scared of going back to jail. That didn't change the fact that I was terrified of what he would do to me if we were around eachother, so Jeryn was returning the favor and letting me stay in her spare bedroom, just until I could get my locks changed. Also, there had been a major development while I had been out of commission.

Apparently, an "anonymous" source called 9-1-1 to report that Axl had actually been the one to assault Jeidyn, not an associate of his like the police had originally thought. When they found and arrested him, Jersei was with him so we were leaving the hospital and going straight to the police station to collect her from child welfare services. Our only step now was to get Drayven home, so that my sister could have her little family altogether. According to the nurses, he was doing so well that we would have a date for him to come home by the end of the week.

The police clearly felt some type of way about my sister beating her charge because all we got was side-eyed as we strolled into the police station. We had no worries. We weren't stressed about it though. Jeryn had been talking about Jersei all morning and after not seeing her for almost two months, the excitement was written all over her face. My sister and I had been planning the surprise party for almost a week, and I couldn't wait to see Jersei's face when she saw unicorn decorations adorning the whole house. Her, Jeidyn and Dom had spent the entire morning decorating the whole house in anticipation for Jersei to come back.

Axl's brothers were at the police station when we walked into the office to gather up Jersei and the looks on their faces said everything. They couldn't believe I was alive. I should have been scared, but I wasn't. Trill wasn't talking to me at the moment, but that didn't mean he didn't have eyes on me. As soon as my sister and I stepped out of this place, there would be twenty soldiers' eyes on us, just waiting for one of the Bailey brothers to make the wrong move. Besides, I was no fool and nobody would ever catch me slacking again. I failed Ezrah, but I wouldn't fail this one. I still couldn't decide on a name for him, because I was so caught up on the loss of my Ezrah. As Jeryn grabbed ahold of Jersei's hand, we both looked around the room and waited for someone to object us taking her home. But the bravery that they had just a week prior was gone, and they all looked around sheepishly. "Pussies," I thought to myself as we walked out of the room. Just as I thought, Trill's boys were everywhere. They didn't even make an attempt to blend in and as we passed them, they all greeted me politely. Even with Trill and I not on good terms, he still made sure that I was good and that meant the world to me. Before I could enjoy Jersei's welcome home party, I needed to have a conversation with my man. I was grown enough to admit that. I had a lot of stuff I needed to get off my chest and I could only imagine that he did too, so I shot him a text to see where he was at and he quickly responded back. I was sure that he wasn't making a play, so I picked up the phone to call him. I was about to hang up but the nervousness I felt turned into butterflies when Trill's baritone voice bellowed through the speaker. I could sense that he was still upset with me, but at least, he was talking to me. That was a start. I was so focused on the puddle settling in my panties, courtesy of his voice, that I forgot I had actually called him for something. I didn't come back to Earth until he began calling my name, over and over again.

"Hmm?" I questioned as I focused on him again. He chuckled slightly, almost like he could read my mind, but he didn't say anything.

"What did you call me for, Eryanna?" he questioned sternly and I gulped, a large lump settling in my throat. I wasn't expecting his mood to go left so quickly, but that didn't stop me from saying what I had to say. Whether or not Trill wanted to hear it, I was about to give him a cold dose of the truth. He could play the silent game with me all he wanted to. At some point, we'd have to be adults and have a real conversation about this.

"Because you're still my baby daddy, Trei Alfred Monroe. If I hadn't been stupid in thinking I was invincible and couldn't be touched, we would have two sons. But I made a mistake, and I have to live with the fact that I didn't protect my son. I'm sorry, Trei, I swear I am. But regardless of the mistake I made, and trust me I'm grown enough to admit I fucked up, we still have one child to raise. One son that is still here with us and he needs both of his parents." I responded. I wasn't rude at all about it, and just by the fact that Trill let out a long breath of air, I knew he was going to agree with me. He hated when I was right.

The line was quiet for a little while, but then Trill finally spoke..

"Move in with me, Ery." He suggested, even though it didn't sound like a suggestion. It sounded like an order that he had said gently. He liked his space and he liked his girl to have her own space as well. That way, he wouldn't have to worry about someone in his face all the time. I shook my head, wanting to make sure I wasn't dreaming but I knew the truth. In all honesty, the shooting had taken a toll on Trill, just like it had done with me, and moving in with him was the only way to keep him sane. Or at least, that was the only way for him to keep tabs on me to make sure I wasn't doing anything crazy. I struggled to find the words to say, but Trill seemed to know exactly what was going through my mind. "I thought I lost you, Eryanna. The baby, I can handle. I can make it through that. I know it sounds fucked up, but we can always have another baby. I can't lose you, Eryanna. I'll go crazy. Being with you has saved me from putting a lot of niggas on their asses and if I lose you, I'm going to turn right into the savage Trill that everyone else knows. You've never had to see that side of me, because I love you and I don't want you to fear me. I don't know what made you so different from these other bitches Ery, but I want all the smoke when it comes to you. These hoes can't compare and I'll air one of these niggas out for trying to take you away from me… but you can't be out here acting wreckless and not at least letting me know what is going on. Come on now. You wouldn't like if I did that shit to you." Trill was never the type to express his feelings so I listened in amazement as he poured his heart out. After a couple of silent moments, Trill finally spoke up again. "I'm sorry for not being there to protect you and my son, Eryanna." He confessed. It bothered me that he blamed himself for something that was entirely my fault. I knew that there was about two hours before Jersei's party started and since Trill was coming anyways, it only seemed right to ride with him.

"Where are you, Trill? I need to see you. I need you to hold me." I disclosed. Yes, I considered myself to be pretty prideful, but this was no longer about me. To be honest, I just needed to feel Trill's arms around me, protecting me and our son from all danger. Trill laughed, and I could tell he was smiling from ear to ear.

"You know where I'm at, crybaby. Come home. We got a lot of making up to do."

# Chapter Nineteen:

*"It really ain't shit to come touch a nigga." -
JayDaYoungan*

My bail was only set at $900,000, thanks to the dumb-ass prosecutor thinking I was one of these other broke niggas out here. My mother came to bail me out within an hour of my bail being posted and I walked out of the holding cell, dapping up each of my brothers as they gave me a hug and Jaxn nodded at me, giving me the signal that what I'd asked him to do while I was gone, was done. When I found out that the state was giving Jersei back to her mama, instead of letting her stay at my parents' house, I refused to just let my daughter go like that. So Jaxn gave Jersei back because he had to, but he'd also placed a location device in the small duffle bag that held all of her clothes. By the end of the night, I was determined to get my baby back. Jeryn and anyone else who stood in my way, was going to die.

So much of my family was at the jailhouse that we automatically had to split up into groups just so that we could all get home. I immediately followed Jaxn to his car, along with two of my other brothers, so that we could discuss the next part of our plan. Pulling the app up on his phone to see Jersei's location, Jaxn handed it to me as I put it into the GPS system. Few people drove around in burgundy BMW's, decked out with rims and speakers that made the whole street shake as he drove, so I recognized J3's car anywhere. Before I could speak up, Jaxn was speeding past him, so I didn't say anything. Contrary to whatever Jeryn believed, there was one person in her family that I actually liked and that was J3. He was the only one of those niggas whose moves ever made sense. The rest of them could suck my dick. I looked behind us but didn't see J3, so I assumed that meant he'd turned at the light. That meant he didn't see us, and I let out a sweet breath of relief. Jeryn and Eryanna did a lot of talking, but their big brother was really about that action and I knew he had no problem killing me and everyone around me. If it was my time to go, it just was, but I didn't want my family involved. My brother turned at the next light and just as he was about to turn on our street, I heard loud popping noises and immediately our car started swerving. I got over the initial shock of being shot at and laid down after our windows shattered. Jaxn did his best to push his foot down on the gas and get us the fuck out of there and it worked. But eventually, J3's car caught up to us and he continued to light our asses up, not even giving us a chance to shoot back. I didn't realize anything was wrong until one of my other brothers began to call Jaxn's name and he wasn't responding. He didn't say anything. Taji, one of my other brothers nudged him. The car slowed down. I looked in the front seat to see my brother slouched over the steering wheel with a bullet in his head. My two other brothers shared a look and then got out of the car to try their chances in running. That didn't stop the bullets and soon after, they were both on the ground as well. I closed my eyes and stayed in the car like a pussy as I prayed that he would pass over me. The karma coming my way wouldn't let that happen. I saw J3's shadow staring at me through the window, but I was frozen and couldn't move. I couldn't even look up at him. I had always been the aggressor. I never had to worry about being shot, because I was the shooter. But the tables had turned and I could only pray that God would spare my life. If he did, I promised him I would be a better man. As if God himself was now sending me a message, I heard J3 laughing and that cut off my prayer. He seemed to look past me and that only made him laugh harder.

"Damn, my nigga! You really pissed on yourself?" he scowled as I looked down to see that I laying in a puddle of my own waste. "My nigga, I should just put you out your misery. I feel bad for you, G." J3 taunted. It was starting to get dark so I knew he wasn't worried about attracting attention. He didn't even check to make sure he was alone. But he reminded me of myself in a lot of ways, and I wouldn't have cared either. Not in a situation like this one. "I can't even do you like this." He confessed and as quickly as I watched his face soften, it hardened back up again. That's when I knew. He didn't care at all about what happened to me. "Sit up." He demanded. I remained still for a moment but eventually, I sat up and that's when J3 cocked his gun. I knew my end had come. Then he pulled the trigger.

# *Chapter Twenty:*

*"I'ma be the bigger man just like I always be." –J. Cole*

*Are you sure you got everything?* Trill's text annoyed me and I fought hard not to roll my eyes while Eryanna was sitting right next to me. She could read me like a book and if she just happened to look over onto the screen of my phone, the entire surprise would be over. Either that or she would think some weird shit was going on. Trill would definitely kill me then. Only a week had passed since Eryanna and Jeidyn came home, but everything seemed to change. Not only was Eryanna moving out of her place, she was moving into Trill's. I was happy for her. It seemed that the two of them were really working to overcome the heartache of losing Ezrah and I couldn't have been prouder. A lot of couples didn't survive miscarriages, let alone one of their unborn babies being shot and killed. I felt so guilty for that but all I could do now was make sure that shit never happened again. Not only were Trill and Eryanna surviving, but Trill was going to ask my sister to marry him. If she said yes, the wedding would also take place today. I had done everything to make sure that the day would be smooth and everything my baby sister deserved. I hired the musicians, confirmed the playlist, ordered the food and flowers, and even had a preacher on standby for when she said yes. The garden that Trill had chosen for the location was beautiful, so I had to make sure that her dress was just as beautiful. I picked out something flattering, but not tight enough that she wouldn't be able to breathe and it was a pretty cream color. Not white. Eryanna hated wearing white and because I could hear her mouth running about dressing her like a virgin, the dress only passed her knees. I couldn't wait to see the look on her face when she realized that him and I had actually done something together that didn't involve us bickering.

As much as I wanted to ignore him, I answered Trill. I knew that if I didn't, he would just blow my phone up and since there was only two hours until I had to meet up with him, I didn't want to give him a reason to freak out. I gave him the go-ahead that our plan was good to go. We were getting our hands and feet done, but I was starting to shake nervously because the Asians were taking longer than usual and at this rate, we would never get to where we needed to go in time. I glanced at my toes every few minutes to check on the progress, and huffed in irritation when I realized she was basically coating the same toe over and over again. Right when I was about to start snapping, Eryanna nudged me. I thought she was just trying to play mediator… until I watched her finger point right at the TV screen. My jaw dropped when I saw Jaxn's car right in the middle of the intersection, shot up like one of Scarface's victims. The news' reporter had arrived at the scene while the cars were still smoking. All I could do was watch in horror at the headlines.

*"Three people are dead and four are in critical condition at Lower Keys tonight after a deadly shooting at the intersection of Fleming and Whitehead. We don't know much right now except three cars were involved and only one car is suspected to have been the shooter. Police are still investigating what happened to cause this tragedy, but they believe that the motive could have stemmed from a war between two families. They're asking the public to please help identify the shooter, who we now have a picture of from the surveillance cameras at the intersection. If you know this man, you're urged to call 9-1-1. He's considered armed and extremely dangerous."* Axl and his family were no strangers to enemies, and they'd made their share just during the time I knew them, so I was expecting to see a familiar face pop up on the screen. But never in a million years would I have expected to see my big brother.

# *Chapter Twenty-One:*

*"Still a call away for the ones who really knew me most." –
Rick Ross*

J3 called Jeryn as we were on our way home, with half-wet toes still and cotton now attached to our cuticles. We'd hauled ass out of there after paying the people, because we knew that we needed to make it to our brother. We even went so far as to call Bellah, who was on her way to meet us as soon as I told her what was going on. There was safety amongst numbers and with J3 having successfully taken out two members of the Bailey cartel and wounded enough of the others that there was no question in our minds that people would be after him. With us however, he was safe because there was no limits to what we would do to keep him safe. That was our big brother but sometimes, even the older siblings needed saving and we wouldn't dare leave J3 out in the cold, to be eaten by the wolves. If going hard for yourself wasn't an option, our dad had taught us, going hard for eachother had to be. Nobody could love you like family, and at this point, family was all we had. I felt bad because I knew that today was supposed to be Eryanna's big day, but that would have to be postponed until I could figure out what to do about our brother. Luckily for me, Trill agreed that we had bigger fish to fry and decided to hold off on proposing with everything going on around us. It felt bittersweet to celebrate a united future together when J3 was feeling like he had just signed his own death certificate. I would make sure the proposal still happened if it was the last thing I did, but it would just have to be after we were completely sure that J3 was safe anywhere else but here.

Our father had taught us a routine growing up for when things went left. As J3 was entering our house, Eryanna and I had already the bags packed, along with any other documentation he would need to get out and quickly. Just by the look on his face, I could tell he was all fucked up behind what he did. But I knew my brother, and if he had to do the same thing over and over to protect us, he would. That's why I loved him. "We gotta leave. Now." J3 demanded as Eryanna and I glanced at eachother in confusion, neither one of us knowing what the fuck was going on. He was supposed to go by himself. Usually, I would ask enough questions to make him want to fight me, but the look on his face told me that there would be no debate here. He had no intentions of arguing with me and us leaving wasn't optional. Already having a couple of duffle bags stashed away in my closet for emergencies like this, I quickly packed up a few last minute things and then put my babies in the car.

To be clear, I wasn't afraid for myself. I could handle myself. The Bailey family was definitely going to come for their revenge and when they did, they were going to knock down everything standing in their way. I couldn't have my kids involved in that, so we followed the plan to a T. J3 and Eryanna were going to take my girls back to Ohio with them since Ery was pregnant and couldn't do much here anyways. Trill and his boys, along with Dom and his soldiers would stay here with me to handle the issue. Drayven though, was going to stay with me because I wasn't sure my breasts could handle him being away from me so long. I had just settled into the breastfeeding thing and the constant need for him to nurse was dragging me, but the connection between us was unlike anything I had with my two girls. I would cry if he had to leave me too.

J3 was on the phone with Bellah as we pulled out of the parking lot and I texted our backup to meet us at the designated place. We knew to involve decoy cars. We had bodyguards traveling in between us, but that didn't help put us at ease as J3 bobbed and weaved through traffic to get us to Bellah and her kids. We also had emergency nannies put in place for things like this, so Eryanna would be alright with all five of the kids, and Bellah agreed to stay here to help me.

With everyone looking out for J3, it wasn't safe for him to stay here and help us fight. Bellah hadn't been exposed to the streets like this before, so she was less prepared than us, but I intended to show her the ropes and get to know her at the same time. Two heads were always better than one, but four heads are always better than three and with the right training, Bellah could join right beside us in running the January empire. I still had yet to see or hear from Jerymiah character, but until he made himself known, I wouldn't worry about it.

Chapter Twenty-Two:



I pulled my baby's pacifier out of his mouth to see if he was really sleeping but quickly put it back and began to rock him when I watched his bottom lip poke out like he was about to cry. I was so excited to have him home after all this time and now we were doing something that would have meant a lot to Jalen. I smiled sadly because though my baby was yellow as fuck like me, he was basically the spitting image of Jalen. They slept the same way and when I woke Drayven up from sleeping, he balled his hands up like he wanted to fight. Just like his daddy used to do. On the two month anniversary of their father's death, I waited outside of his mother's home for someone to open the door while I held my two kids. I knew there were people inside, because I could hear them. After going back and forth on the issue in my mind, I knew that my kids needed to meet their father's side of the family. Since he wasn't alive anymore, that was the only connection they had left to him. I wasn't close to my side so literally all my kids had were their aunts and uncle. I wanted them to have more than that. They deserved it. Besides, Jalen would have wanted them to meet Drayven so I intended to honor him in any way that I could. Had I not insisted that Jeidyn be kept a secret from his family, he would have flaunted his baby girl proudly. I found myself having to shake away my feelings as I watched my beautiful baby boy suck on his fingers to comfort himself and go back to sleep. He didn't deserve this. He didn't deserve any of this and it was all my fault, but I intended to make it right by him and his sister if it was the last thing I did. When the door finally swung open and Jalen's older sister's hateful eyes stared back at me, I should have turned around, headed back to my car and drove off. But I didn't. My feet didn't get the notice from my brain to stand down and they were frozen in place while I stammered, struggling and searching for the right words to say. My mouth had become dry like I swallowed a handful of cottonballs.

"Can I help you?" she asked, getting straight to the point. By the venom in her voice, I could tell that she already knew exactly who I was. That probably meant she already knew exactly why I was there. Even still, I decided to do the polite thing and introduce myself. Just due to the nature of Jalen and I's relationship and the importance of discretion between us, I had never met any of his family in person. But

I had seen lots of pictures that made me feel like I was a part of his family. Other than Eryanna, Jalen had never met anyone in my family either. We had decided in the beginning of our "arrangement" that in order to control the nature of our relationship, we needed to control who all knew about us. We didn't go on public dates and if we happened to be at the same event, we stayed far enough away from each other that nobody would find it suspicious. If we needed to see eachother, I'd make up an excuse for a trip and Jalen and I would link in another city. One of Axl's bodyguards was usually always with me so Jalen and I depended on trips with my sister and Trill, and late-night sneaky link ups to get our fill of one another. With Axl always being gone or out of town on business, it was usually easy enough to sneak away for a little while.

"Hi, you must be Kayla. You don't know me-," I began. I shut up almost immediately when she began to suck her teeth and roll her eyes.

"How could I forget the woman who barged in on my brother's wedding?" She snapped, glaring me down as she folded her arms. "He told us the situation… He told us way after the fact that you two have a daughter." Kayla started to explain before she had to stop and gather her emotions. I watched as she stole a peek of the bundle burrowing itself further into my chest. I ran my hands over his silky, black hair.

"Yes, we have a daughter. We have a son too. This is Drayven. He was born the day that Jalen died." I introduced. The smile on my face was undeniable and I wasn't paying any attention to the doubt written all over Kayla's face. At the end of the day, I knew exactly who my son's father was and that was Jalen Louis Hicks. I knew people would have their doubts because my skin was the color of burnt peanut butter and Jalen was a beautiful milk chocolate color. But Drayven looked like a little mixed baby and I couldn't explain it. Genetics just worked in mysterious ways, I guess. Kayla continued to stay silent while she stared at my son.

"Jeryn, I know exactly who you are. I just don't know why you're here." Kayla responded coldly and I felt tears springing to my eyes. I knew I deserved that reaction, but my children didn't. Usually, I would have just brushed her comments off but I was already a wreck. Between post-partum hormones and still healing, I was an emotional mess and Kayla wasn't making it any better. I tried to swallow the knot in my throat when I saw her check to make sure nobody else was coming to the door. "Before you, my brother was happy and alive. Now, he's dead. He died visiting you. There is nothing you could say that would make me feel better. You should go now." Without letting me say anything to defend myself, Kayla shut the door in my face and left me standing there like a fool. For the first time in all of my life, I had nothing to say.

# *Chapter Twenty-Three:*

*"I found out you was shady though." -Dreezy*

After hearing the security system activate itself for the fourth time that night, Trill and I watched on high alert, holding our breaths as we waited for something to happen. That was how it had been for the past three weeks since my sisters and brother had left. Still, nothing had popped off. Two members of the Bailey family had just been released from the hospital, which I knew because I had been watching the news. It took everything in me not to gag when I saw their names and faces pop up on my TV, but I knew what their releases meant. The battle was just getting started so we had to be ready for whatever. But as time passed and Eryanna got closer to the delivery date of her child, I could tell that Trill was getting antsy to have her back home and I was missing my girls. We were both just looking forward to this being over with so that we could move on with our lives.

But once again, for the 20th consecutive night, here I was running my fingers through my son's thick coils as I stared out of the window, just waiting for something to rub me the wrong way. A jogger that paused in front of my house too long, or a car that turned into my driveway and then went the opposite way. That's stuff you see every day, right? Well it's never a threat until your life is in danger. Trill stood in the corner, watching quietly like he often did. We had been secluded together for almost an entire month, and yet we hardly ever talked. That was okay though, because Trill and I preferred it that way. This time was different, and I could tell Trill had something important on his mind. I could tell just by the way that he stared off into space. After I was sure that Drayven was fast asleep, I swaddled him up, made sure his pacifier was in his mouth and then laid him down in his crib, kissing him goodnight. I did all that knowing that by the end of the night, he would still end up in the bed next to me. Trill walked behind me as we went out onto the deck to smoke a blunt. I had never really considered myself a pothead, but these were unusual times for me and smoking was the only thing that helped to ease my mind. Even if it was just for a moment. We'd established a routine so once we headed out, Trill knew what time it was and had the blunts already rolled and ready to light up. By the time we hit the door, he was firing that bitch up.

"So what's good? And don't say nothing either because you've been sitting there like you have a stick up your ass, all day." I asked, watching the smoke trail up my nose as Trill still said nothing. I hit it a couple of times before passing it back to Trill. Instead of actually hitting the blunt, he just stared straight ahead.

"Jeryn, you know that thing we put off right?" Trill asked and I chuckled. Trill was so scared of commitment that he couldn't even say wedding. "Can you get your sister back here this weekend? I'm ready." He asked and I swallowed the knot in my throat. I loved love, but bringing Eryanna back right now wasn't a smart idea. Not while we were in the middle of a retaliation war. The Bailey's already wanted Eryanna's head on a stick and I wasn't going to risk her losing her life. Trill must have already been reading my mind and knew exactly what I was going to say because when he passed the blunt back, he grabbed my wrist and forced me to look him dead in his eyes. "I'm serious, Jeryn. I'll do whatever you want me to do but I'm ready for Eryanna to be my wife and I can't wait any longer. I won't let nothing bad happen to her, just let her come back. Call anybody you need to so you can pull this off. Your sister will be Eryanna Monroe by Sunday." If I had any doubt in my mind before then, Trill erased it all in that moment and I couldn't help the tear that slipped out of my eyes. My baby sister had really found love.

"I have a better idea, Trill. I don't know if bringing

her here is the safest… so let's go there."

# Chapter Twenty-Four:

Things had slowly started to fizzle out once we left, and since we'd landed in Ohio, I hadn't heard any noise from the Bailey's. That was over a week ago and I was sure that we were in the clear now. Or at least, there wouldn't be anything we couldn't handle so I packed my entire family up and took us back to the Keys. I should have known that was just the calm before a storm.

Dressing Drayven up in the cutest outfit I could find him, I made sure that both of the girls and I looked presentable and then I loaded us all up into the car. I thought it was hard with two but with three, it was nearly impossible. If this moment hadn't been so important, I would have stayed at home but I needed to take advantage of this downtime. With it not being so hot in the streets any more, I felt like it was safe for my kids to go out. That meant before I did anything else, I needed to take my son to meet his father. I pulled up into the cemetery and goosebumps immediately showed up all over my neck and arms. I hated the cemetery. Knowing that Jalen would be my final stop there, I gave Jeidyn and Jersey both a bouquet of flowers while I somehow managed to balance holding the third bouquet in one hand while balancing Drayven on my hip with the other. My first stop was to see my parents. Though Eryanna took pride in going to see our parents' gravesites regularly, or at least she had, I hadn't been here since we buried our father and I had to accept that my sister and I were now orphans and left to fend for ourselves. Aside from my post-pregnancy hormones, I still considered myself to be grieving over the loss of my parents so I knew this would be interesting. I first stopped at my mom's tombstone, wiping away the dust and the old leaves as my tears gave her nameplate its own personal bath.

"I miss you so much mommy," I paused, trying to both contain myself and rock Drayven, who was starting to trip out on me. "This isn't the same without you. Life isn't the same without you… The girls remind me so much of you, mommy. Especially Jeidyn. You would be crazy about them, but I'm sure you know that already since you picked them out for me. Your grandson, too…" I began to cry again, so I took a break. "I don't hate you for what you did, mommy. No matter what Eryanna or anyone else thinks. I just hate that you left and I didn't get a chance to say goodbye. I'm sorry that we made life so hard for you. I'm sorry that we weren't worth fighting for. I loved you more than the air that I breathed, mommy…" Knowing that I didn't want to push my luck and risk the chance of someone seeing me, I gave my mom's tombstone a quick kiss and then had Jersey place a bouquet there. Then, I walked next to my mother's tomb stone and as my father's name jumped out at me, I could feel the rage swelling up inside of me. "Daddy, thank you…" I kept it simple. Now that my girls were older, they understood more and I didn't want to be that person. Besides, if he could actually hear me, he knew what I was thanking him for. He had ruined my life but I couldn't bring myself to disrespect the dead so I motioned for Jeidyn to place her bouquet down as well so that we could move on. I was doing so well, right until we found the tombstone of Jalen Louis Hicks. Reading his name up there, enshrined like that, just did something to me and I began to cry inconsolably. I cried for over ten minutes before I realized that I needed to pull myself together. Not for myself, but for my kids who were watching me suffer and unable to do anything to help me. I cried until I couldn't produce any more tears and then I wiped my face and began to talk. I wasn't sure if my mom could hear me. I didn't know if my dad could hear me. But I was a hundred-percent positive that Jalen could. I could feel it deep in my spirit. "I finally got it together, Jalen. I finally named our son. I thought I couldn't do it without you, but I'm doing it for you. This is Drayven Louis January. I was going to let him be a Hicks, but I didn't know how your people would react to that." I laughed, shutting up when I realized inside jokes weren't as funny with just one person there. "I'm sure you know this, but Dray looks so much like you. He even sleeps like you. Thank you for giving me two little pieces of you before you left me." I said honestly, smiling when I looked over at Jeidyn. She was still so little but something told me that she knew exactly what was going on. Or at least she had an idea. Placing his bunch of flowers on the ground near his name, I leaned over to kiss his tombstone. Then I placed Drayven's hand there since that would be the closest thing to touching his father that he would ever get. I heard someone clear their throat and when I looked up, I was surprised to see Kayla, Jalen's oldest sister, standing there. I had all three of my children with me and I wasn't trying to cause a scene at Jalen's resting place.

"You shouldn't be here." She scolded me as I stood up. If it was a fight she wanted, she wouldn't get it from me. Not here and not while I had my babies with me. I grabbed Jeidyn by the hand as I held Drayven on my hip. I walked past Kayla and she grabbed me by the shoulder. I almost let go of my daughter's hand and swung on her, but then I noticed the look in her eyes. It wasn't anger or hatred. It wasn't her being struck on revenge. It was a look of pure concern. "Look, Jeryn. I may not like you. Actually, I don't think I've hated anyone as much as I hate you but none of that matters. You need to watch your back. You need to leave. I'm not sure if you know this, but you've made an enemy I'm not sure you can handle and everyone is talking about it… You and your family are in danger, Jeryn… and that includes my niece and nephew." I thought about asking her what threat she was referring to, but it was better for both of us if I didn't play dumb. My heart was pounding as Kayla's words replayed in my head, over and over again. I was practically sprinting with my kids to the car. I had thought everything was cool now, but it didn't seem like that was the case so I knew I had to do the right thing. I had to make sure my family was safe, above everything else. I put my keys in the ignition, after fumbling for awhile, and then I sped off and got as far away from the cemetery as I could. All I could do was pray that there were no police behind me because I burned rubber all the way back to Eryanna's house. I got all of my kids out and then hustled us all to the door as I unlocked it, all the while watching our backs. It was late so I wasn't surprised when everyone was asleep, and I decided to just let them rest. I knew that it would be awhile before they got another good night's sleep.

# Chapter Twenty-Five:

With everyone all together in the huge house that Trill had rented for us under his mother's name, I felt comfortable in knowing that my brother, sisters, nieces and nephew were safe. Trill had people posted outside so I knew nobody was getting in here, but if for any reason they did, we had a bunch of guns hidden around the house and I had no problem with using one. Nobody would ever catch me slipping again.

The only thing that I hated about being with so many people was that every time I heard a footstep or a creak in the floorboards, I would wake all the way up and wait in agony for someone to break in and kill us all. So when I heard the front door open and close at nearly three o'clock in the morning, I held my breath and waited for the inevitable end. Nothing happened so I creeped down the stairs and headed to the door to check out what was going on. I had my favorite piece in my hand, ready for whatever. I thought about just opening the door to start spraying, but I didn't want to be ambushed while I was down here by myself. However, all of those thoughts went away as I checked out of the peephole and saw Dom and Bellah, sitting outside and talking. I relaxed, knowing there was no threat to me but then as I walked towards the kitchen for a late-night snack, I overheard their conversation.

"You need to tell her, Dom. That's not right." Bellah scolded him, as I prepared to confront them both. Being the hothead that I was, my first thought was that he was cheating on my sister but then I continued to eavesdrop.

"Bellah, man, you know how hard I worked to get that woman to trust me. If I tell her this, I'll lose her forever and I can't do that."

"Maybe, but can you really sleep next to her, knowing what you did? What if she finds out a different way? You know the streets talk." Bellah explained as I found myself growing angrier with her. It seemed that her loyalty was with Dom and not our sister. That was a problem for me.

"Bellah, I swear to God that none of this shit was supposed to happen. I just did what you asked me to do." That's when my eyes bulged. Was this really happening? Were they really saying what I thought they were saying?

"Whoa, whoa, whoa. Dominique, you know I never asked you to kill Jalen. I asked you to kill Jeremih. You got the wrong person. That's not my fault." She scolded as I struggled to pull my jaw off of the floor. I was about to walk away and escape quietly but the floor creaked and Bellah and

Dom both stopped talking.

"Fuck." I cursed under my breath, realizing I was trapped. When she peeked in, I thought I was caught but I played it off quickly. "I thought I heard the door open. You almost got shot." I half-lied, smiling as I waved my piece before going back upstairs with my gun. I knew that I'd have to tell Jeryn but I didn't want to wake her up, especially since she had just gotten Dray to sleep. The news would have to wait until the morning. I just wondered how she would take it.

# Chapter Twenty-Five:

*"So fuck that cuffin' shit." –Wale ft. Jeremih*

Sneaking into the bed to give Dom a kiss on his cheek, I kissed his neck and laughed when he gripped me by the ass. He mumbled something into my neck but I couldn't hear what he was saying. His breath against my neck tickled so I shivered and pulled away. Despite the physical connection, I couldn't take it there with him. I was just preparing myself for the worst and giving him all of me would only result in it hurting me a lot worse. That didn't mean I didn't want to. God, I wanted to. Just sitting there and watching him sleep sometimes made me want to lick his face and all the other parts of him as well. I had never expected to fall like this but Dom had caught me off guard and I was loving every moment of it. Being around him almost made me forget that there was a hit out on my head and I knew I couldn't continue to put his life in danger. I cared about him too much for that and I would never be able to live with myself if something happened to Dom because of me and his daughter was left out here, all alone. Reading over the note one last time, I propped it up on the pillow and then left the house, throwing my bags over my shoulder and heading to the car. There were people looking for me everywhere and they knew what my car looked like so when I went into the garage, I grabbed Dom's keys. I had to move fast before I changed my mind and went to crawl back in my bed with my man so I skirted off so fast down the street, I thought I saw smoke.

I only made it about five minutes before Dom started blowing up my phone. I sent him straight to voicemail the first three times, but he didn't give up. I sighed and stared ahead at the road to focus, knowing that the longer I stared, the more possible it would become that I would answer the phone and turn back around. I knew that I would renege on everything I'd told myself in the pep talk that morning and I couldn't have that. He called about five more times and I don't know why, but when he called the sixth time, I picked up the phone.

"H-hello?" I greeted him, trying my best to remain strong.

"Baby, what are you doing?" he asked me and I found myself pulling over to gather myself. It took Dom a few minutes, but then he continued to talk even though I wasn't answering. "Wait, Jeryn. Did you take my car?" he asked seriously, and I prepared for him to cuss me out. Aside from

Diamond, his car was his baby. But he didn't curse at me at all. As a matter of fact, he was dead quiet until he began to beg and plead with me. I barely paid him any mind as I cried until I heard him stop pleading. "Don't talk, Jeryn. Just listen. I need to tell you something. Y-you're not the only one with a-," The sound of his voice was interrupted by my screams when the entire car was shot up. I attempted to drive away but the car only made it a few feet. I could hear numerous people jumping out of their cars but my head was against the steering wheel and all I could see was blood leaking out of me and onto the floor of my car. I could hear a group of people's footsteps getting a lot closer but I wasn't sure if I'd make it to see whether they were coming to save my life, or end it. I started seeing doubles and then my vision blurred completely. As my eyes closed, a single tear fell down my cheek.

"This is it…" I thought to myself.

*To be continued*